SOMNIUM
TERRAM
Where Dreams are Made
Swim with the hyper-realistic Whales
Explore the atmosphere controlled Mountains
Take a Safari in the Authentic™ Wild Jungles
Relax in one of our 750 Themed Casinos
whilst our AI service droids cater for your every need!
YOU DESERVE IT
Seasonal climate controlled environments.
Family and Family-Free zones available
VIV Certified - Virus, Insect & Vermin eradicated
Note: Adventure experiences shown are subject to wealth restrictrictions
PROUD TO BE PART OF
PATRIAM CORPORATION
BUILT FOR YOUR FUTURE

INSPIRED BY
THROUGH THE LOOKING GLASS
BY LEWIS CARROLL (1871)

AL15 2

BROKEN DREAMS

WRITTEN & ILLUSTRATED BY STEVE DE LA MARE

For Markosia Enterprises Ltd

Harry Markos
Publisher & Managing Partner

GM Jordan
Special Projects Co-Ordinator

Andy Briggs
Creative Consultant

Ian Sharman
Editor In Chief

 Published by Markosia Enterprises, PO BOX 3477, Barnet, Hertfordshire, EN5 9HN. FIRST PRINTING, October 2022. Harry Markos, Director.

ISBN 978-1-915387-70-7

www.markosia.com

AL
15

AL15 HAD ARRIVED ON SOMNIUM TERRAM

TO FIND HER WAY HOME TO VIRIDI

A NEW PLANET

THE DRAGON THAT BROUGHT AL15 HERE
SOARED AWAY TO JOIN OTHER SCREECHING CREATURES
THAT WERE CIRCLING OVERHEAD
AND BECAME ONE OF THE MANY

IN THE DISTANCE, LIKE A MIRAGE, COLOSSAL BUILDINGS OF A CITY ROSE UPWARDS TOWARDS THE BURNT SKY WHERE ELECTRIC STORMS RAGED

AL15 HEADED TOWARDS THE MIRAGE
THE SOIL WAS PARCHED. IT WAS AS THOUGH THE WORMHOLE WAS CLASHING VIOLENTLY WITH THE ATMOSPHERE OF THE PLANET AND SINGEING THE VERY GROUND SHE STOOD ON

THIS WAS NOT THE DREAM LAND AL15 WAS EXPECTING

ZUGZWANG MEGALOPOLIS

BACK ON
MIROR TERRAM

YUP THAT IS EXACTLY HOW IT HAPPENED

THERE IS A SHIP APPROACHING. WE ARE GATHERING TO WELCOME THEM
A SHIP! A SHIP IS COMING!
AT LAST! WE FINALLY TAKE OUR PLACE IN THIS MAD UNIVERSE

THIS IS THE FIRST CONTACT WE'VE HAD! I HOPE THEY'RE FRIENDLY
DO WE KNOW WHO THEY ARE?
AS NEW MAYOR I HAVE REHEARSED THE WELCOME. NOW DON'T SCARE THEM OFF..
SAYER, PERHAPS YOU'D BEST STAND AT THE BACK

RELEASE ANDROMEDA LEWIS OR FACE THE CONSEQUENCES!
YOU HAVE TWO MINUTES TO COMPLY

ZUGZWANG MEGALOPOLIS
I COULD HAVE SWORN I SAW SOMEONE RUN PAST JUST THEN
DOESN'T LOOK TOO FRIENDLY!
ZUGZWANG MEGALOPOLIS
EVEN LESS SO NOW!
THREAT

ZUGZWANG MEGALOPOLIS
WOAH! WHAT IS GOING ON?

AL15 REALIZED THE MACHINES WERE NOT JUST FIGHTING OFF THE DRAGONS BUT HAD MADE A SAFETY CORRIDOR TO THE ENTRANCE
HOWEVER THE DRAGONS WEREN'T BACKING-OFF..
..THEY WERE MAKING WAY FOR THE ALPHA

WOAH STEADY ON! I'M SURE WE CAN WORK SOMETHING OUT WE ARE PEACEFUL HERE
ARE YOU SURE YOU HAVE THE RIGHT PLACE?
WHO IS IT YOU ARE LOOKING FOR?
ANDROMEDA LEWIS! FROM VIRIDI I KNOW SHE IS HELD CAPTIVE HERE NOW RELEASE HER!
VIRIDI? WE DON'T KNOW ANYONE FROM VIRIDI DO WE?
NO.. APART FROM AL15
AL15! THAT IS HER! THAT IS ANDROMEDA
OH AL15 ISN'T WITH US ANYMORE
GRUB?
WHAT?! WHAT HAVE YOU DONE WITH HER? IF YOU'VE HURT HER...
NO, NO HE MEANS SHE'S NOT HERE ANYMORE
SHE LEFT. WENT HOME
AL15 DID NOT RETURN!
NOW I'LL ASK ONE MORE TIME..

WHERE
IS
MY DAUGHTER
?

CL
14

I AM CASSIOPEIA LEWIS
ANDROMEDA'S MOTHER
14TH GENERATION
MECH ENGINEER
FROM THE ANT COLONY
VIRIDI TERRAM
CL
14
ANDROMEDA DISAPPEARED
DURING A CELEBRATION
THAT HONORS OUR
FIRST PIONEERS
I'M ONE OF
THOSE PIONEERS
WHAT?
LONG STORY...
FOR ANOTHER TIME
SORRY,
DO GO ON
NO ONE REMEMBERED SEEING HER ALL EVENING
WHEN SHE DIDN'T COME HOME THAT NIGHT
WE SEARCHED EVERYWHERE FOR HER
WE SCOURED THE MOON
& CONTACTED THE OTHER COLONIES
STILL NOTHING
WE HOPED PERHAPS SHE
HAD FOUND A LIFE-PARTNER
AS SHE WAS COMING UP TO
'SETTLING AGE'
BUT SHE WAS NOWHERE
THEY EVEN
DREDGED
THE TANKS

THEN, WHEN WE THOUGHT ALL WAS LOST A COURIER CAME FORWARD
THE QUEEN WAS MY SISTER! ALSO A PIONEER AGAIN, LONG STORY ..ACTUALLY, SAME STORY
HE TOLD US WHAT ILIFE WAS REALLY LIKE ON YOUR MOON & THAT HE WAS FORCED TO LURE ANDROMEDA HERE TO BECOME A PRISONER OF YOUR QUEEN
WHEN WE DISCOVERED THE TRUTH WE BEGGED THE ELDERS TO SEND A SHIP TO RESCUE HER
BUT THEY REFUSED SAYING 'MIROR TERRAM WAS STRICTLY OFF-BOUNDS' & 'BESIDES A SHIP WOULD BE A WASTE OF RESOURCES'
SO I.. BORROWED ONE
AH THAT'S WHERE AL15 GETS IT FROM!

PLEASE, I HAVE TRAVELLED A LONG WAY. I NEED TO FIND HER.
SHE WONT BE ABLE TO COPE BY HERSELF!
ARE YOU SURE YOU'RE TALKING ABOUT THE SAME AL15? THE AL15 WHO BEFRIENDED TIGERS & DRAGONS, FOUGHT OFF HUNTERS AND FREED US FROM OPPRESSION?
I CAN SHOW YOU THE PICTURES?
CASSIOPEIA LISTENED AS *THE ADVENTURES OF AL15* WERE RECOUNTED IN DETAIL
SHE WAS TOLD HOW HER BRAVE DAUGHTER RAN INTO A BLAZING FOREST FOUGHT THE PACK TO SAVE BLEM DEFENDED A STALLHOLDER FREED HERSELF FROM PRISON BEFORE DEFEATING THE QUEEN
& HOW SHE FINALLY RODE A DRAGON THROUGH THE WORMHOLE TO SOMNIUM TO GET HOME
AFTER A LONG SILENCE CASSIOPEIA ASKED IF THEY MIGHT TAKE HER TO THE PLACE WHERE HER DAUGHTER WAS LAST SEEN

GOOD EVENING INSERT MISS LOVELY EVENING FOR A STROLL
LET'S GET YOU BACK INSIDE
SECURITY
NOW YOU DON'T APPEAR TO BE ON OUR L-L-L-LIST
I'M.. NEW HERE I'VE JUST ARRIVED
AH THAT WILL EXPLAIN IT

I'M TRYING TO FIND PASSAGE TO GET BACK HOME TO VIRIDI TERRAM
PLEASE CAN YOU HELP ME?
OF COURSE NOT A PROBLEM JUST STEP INSIDE AND WE'LL SORT YOU OUT RIGHT AWAY-Y-Y
SOMNIUM TERRAM
YOU DESERVE IT
SECURITY
WELL THAT WAS EASY!
WELCOME

OMNIUM TERRAM
NEW YEAR'S EVE CHARITY FUNDRAISER SPECTACULAR!
TONITE
PATRIAM CORPORATION
HEY! WHAT ARE YOU DOING? LET ME OUT!!

IT WAS RIGHT HERE! I KNOW IT WAS HERE BECAUSE THESE METAL CHUNKS FELL THROUGH JUST AFTER AL15 LEFT WEEEEEEEEEEE BOOOOFF!
WAIT, THAT'S NOT CHUNKS OF METAL THAT LOOKS LIKE AN OLD SERVICE DROID!
HAS NO-ONE TRIED TO FIX IT OR EVEN ANALYZE THE DATA?
WE DON'T HAVE THE SKILLS WITH METAL MACHINES
WELL I DO!
HELP ME GET IT BACK TO THE SHIP
I WANT TO SEE WHAT THIS THING CAN TELL US

WEST ENTRANCE LEVEL 1
CAM 103

WEST ENTRANCE STAIRWAY
CAM 107

WEST ENTRANCE LEVEL 2
CAM 20A
WEST ENTRANCE LEVEL 4
CAM 426

EVEN IF YOU CAN GET THIS THING TO WORK HOW CAN IT HELP FIND ALI5? IT ONLY PASSED HER GOING THE OTHER WAY
BECAUSE OF WORMHOLE TIME-LAW
SAY WHAT NOW?
THEORY GOES YOU CAN ONLY TRAVEL BACKWARDS IN TIME THROUGH A WORMHOLE TO A PAST RUPTURE, WHICH HAS BECOME A FIXED EVENT
& ACCORDING TO BASIC TIME-LAW THE DROID HAD TO HAVE BEEN THERE LONGER THAN THE TIME SHE TRAVELLED BACKWARDS FOR IT TO GET HERE WHEN IT DID
I THOUGHT IT WAS ONLY A THEORY. THEY EXPERIMENTED WITH CREATING WORMHOLES BACK ON OLD EARTH
SO THIS DROID MUST HAVE GONE THROUGH IN ALI5'S FUTURE TIMELINE & RE-APPEARED BACK HERE THE MOMENT SHE LEFT.
AGREED?
...YUP

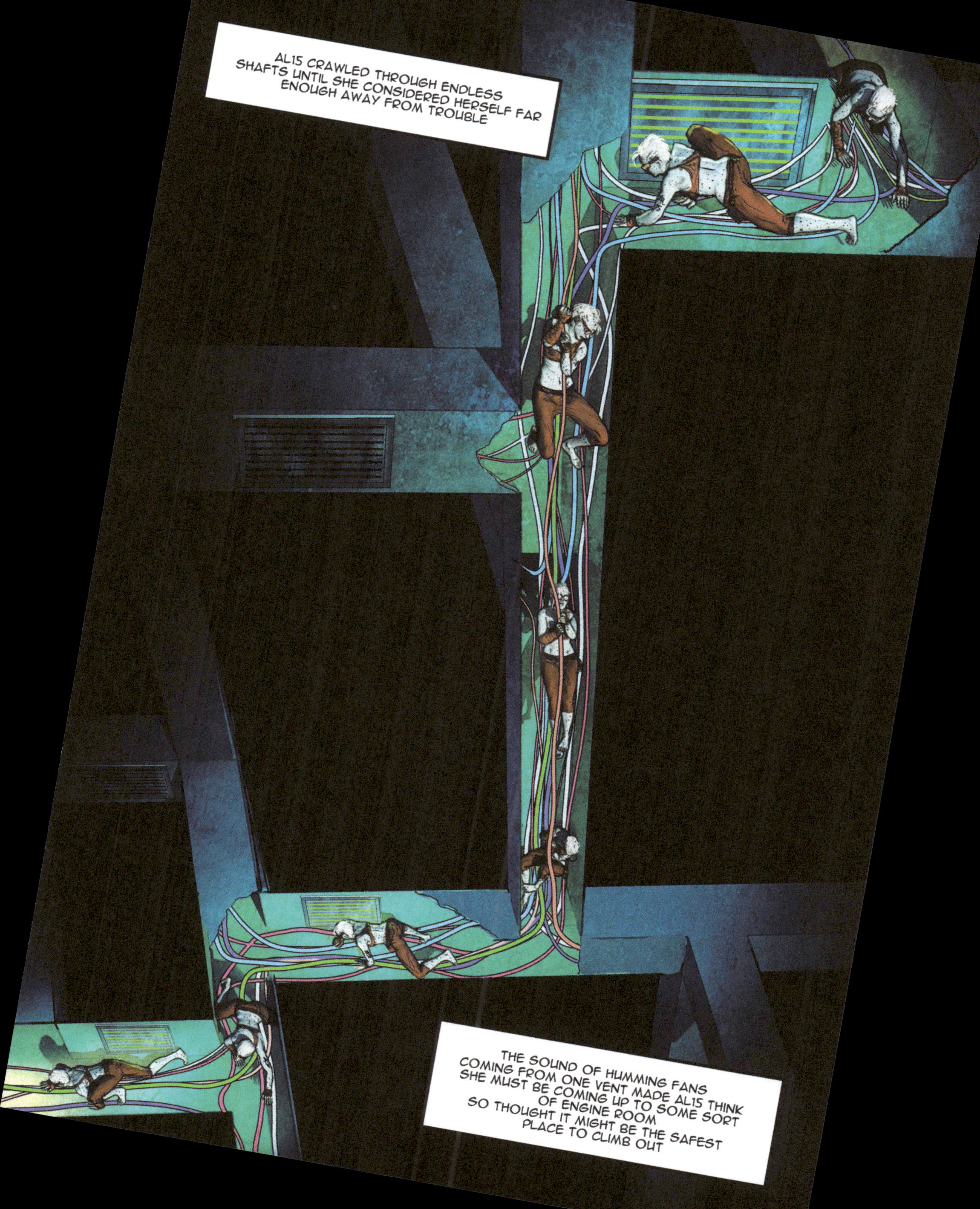
AL15 CRAWLED THROUGH ENDLESS SHAFTS UNTIL SHE CONSIDERED HERSELF FAR ENOUGH AWAY FROM TROUBLE
THE SOUND OF HUMMING FANS COMING FROM ONE VENT MADE AL15 THINK SHE MUST BE COMING UP TO SOME SORT OF ENGINE ROOM SO THOUGHT IT MIGHT BE THE SAFEST PLACE TO CLIMB OUT

DEEP

DEEP
OCEAN

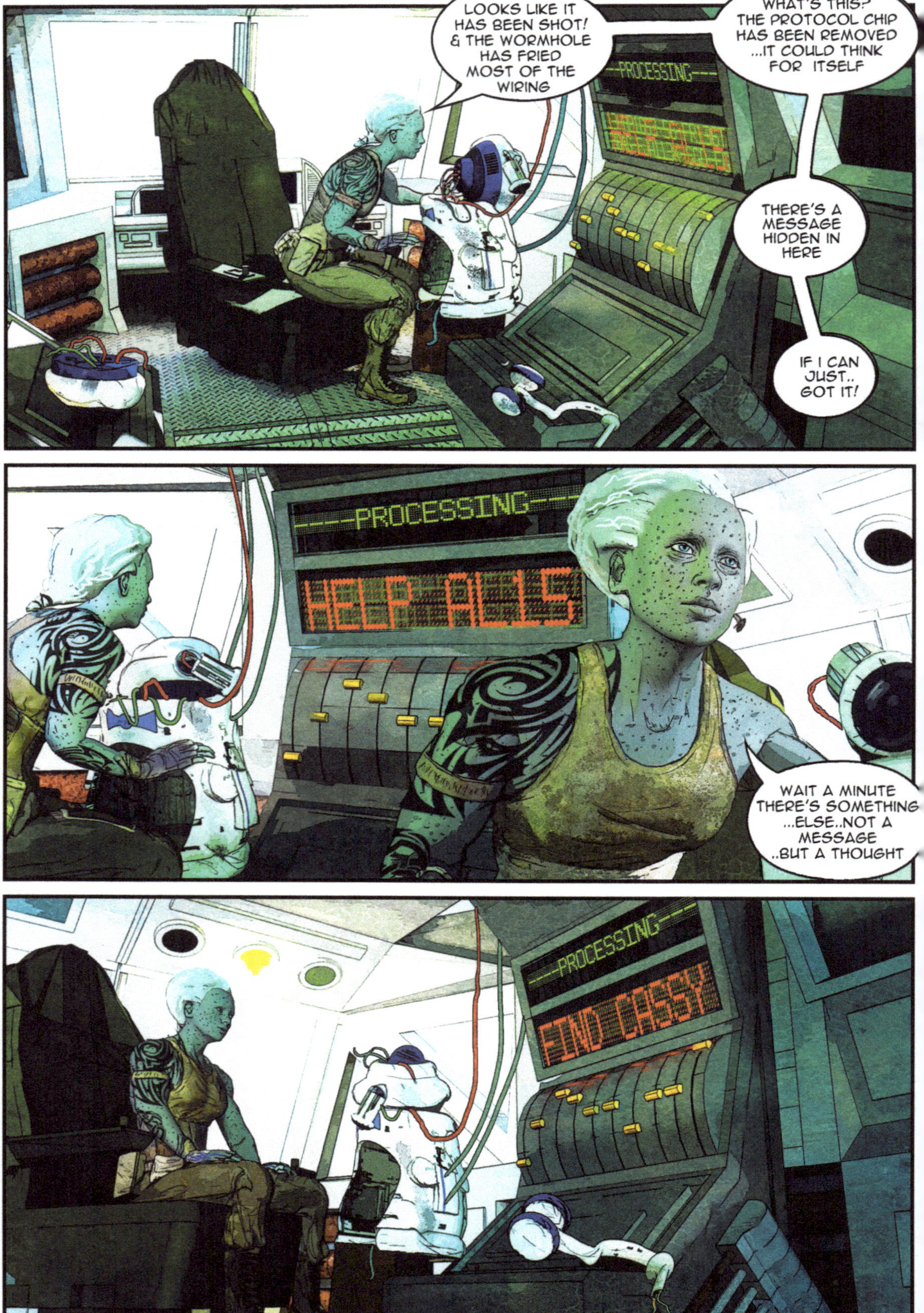
LOOKS LIKE IT HAS BEEN SHOT! & THE WORMHOLE HAS FRIED MOST OF THE WIRING
WHAT'S THIS? THE PROTOCOL CHIP HAS BEEN REMOVED ...IT COULD THINK FOR ITSELF
PROCESSING
THERE'S A MESSAGE HIDDEN IN HERE
IF I CAN JUST.. GOT IT!
PROCESSING
HELP ALIS
WAIT A MINUTE THERE'S SOMETHING ...ELSE..NOT A MESSAGE ..BUT A THOUGHT
PROCESSING
FIND CASSY

WHAT DOES THAT MEAN? IS CASSY A PLACE?
I'M CASSY IT'S WHAT MY FRIENDS CALL ME
WELL, CASSY, HOW WOULD IT KNOW YOUR NAME?
I SAID FRIENDS YOU'RE NOT THERE YET
WHO AM I KIDDING? IT IS NO USE THE JOURNEY WOULD TAKE TOO LONG & WITH THE REVERSE TIMELINE IT MAY ALREADY BE TOO LATE
IT'S NEVER TOO LATE THAT'S MY TIMEHOLE THEORY
WONDERFUL! THEN THAT HAS TO TAKE US BACK TO WHEN THIS DROID LEFT!
THERE'S ONE AT THE MOMENT NOT FAR FROM HERE
OH..THAT'S IT!.. WORMHOLE TELL ME WHEN IS THE NEXT WORMHOLE DUE?
THIS IS IMPORTANT THINK CAREFULLY HAS THERE BEEN ANOTHER ONE SINCE AL15 LEFT?
..NO I DON'T THINK SO
I NEED TO FIX THIS THING PROPERLY IT MAY BE OF USE WE'RE LEAVING VERY SOON

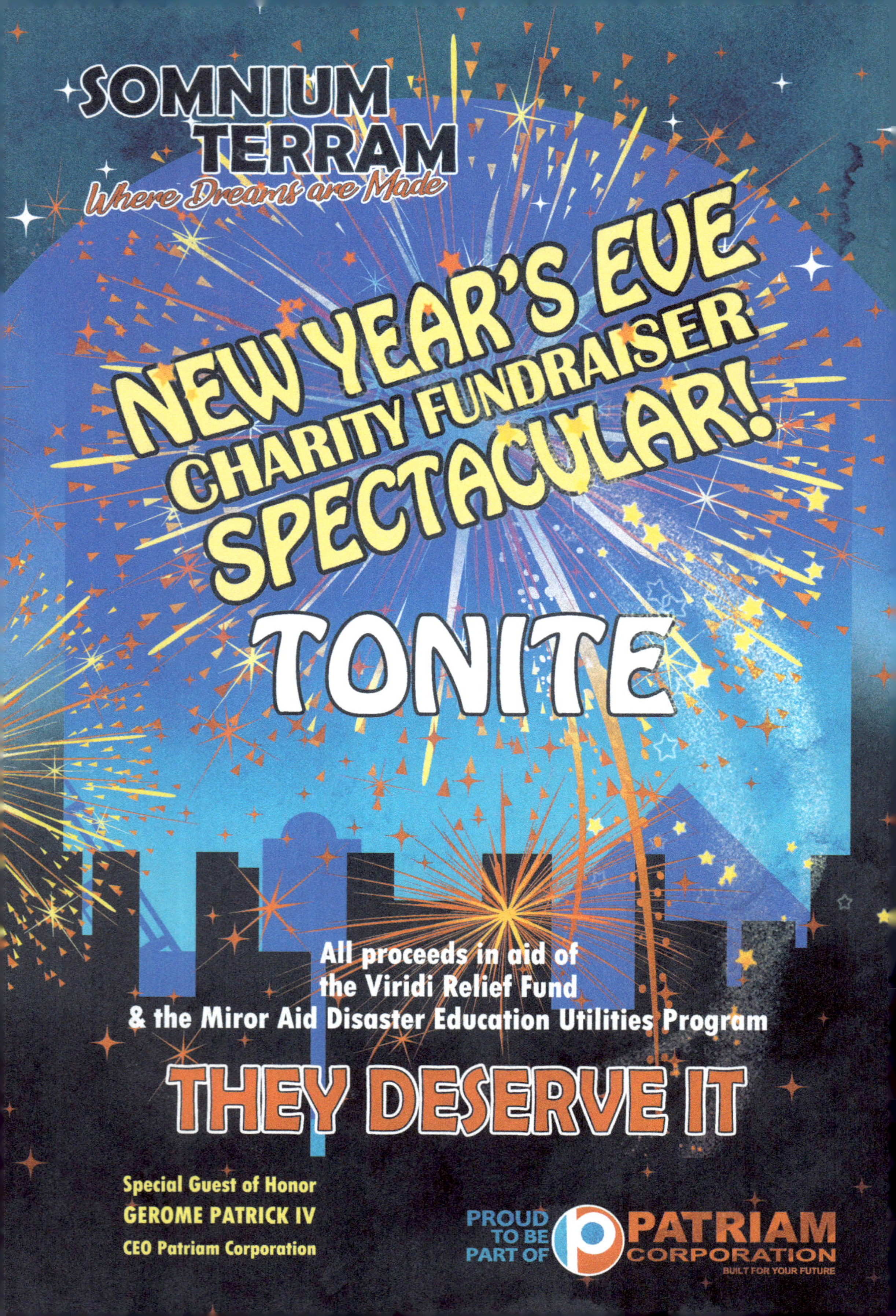
SOMNIUM TERRAM
Where Dreams are Made
NEW YEAR'S EVE
CHARITY FUNDRAISER
SPECTACULAR!
TONITE
All proceeds in aid of
the Viridi Relief Fund
& the Miror Aid Disaster Education Utilities Program
THEY DESERVE IT
Special Guest of Honor
GEROME PATRICK IV
CEO Patriam Corporation
PROUD TO BE PART OF
PATRIAM CORPORATION
BUILT FOR YOUR FUTURE

WHAT THE...?
WHERE AM I?
& MORE IMPORTANTLY
WHY AM I IN THIS STUPID DRESS?!
HOW ARE YOU EVEN SUPPOSED TO WALK IN THIS.. ..THING?!

COOEEE ALIS!
THERE YOU ARE! HIDING IN THE GARDEN AS USUAL
YOU'RE JUST IN TIME FOR THE FIREWORKS! & SUCH A GOOD CAUSE: THOSE POOR STARVING CHILDREN ON VIRIDI
SORRY, WHAT? I'M FROM VIRIDI. NO ONE IS STARVING THERE, WE MAKE FOOD
YES OF COURSE YOU DO DEAR THAT'S NICE
NOW I'VE RESERVED US A PLACE ON THE BALCONY! WORTH EVERY CENT!
THEY SAY GEROME PATRICK IV IS GOING TO BE HERE IN PERSON VIA A LIVE FEED SUCH A DISH.. COULD BE HUSBAND NUMBER 7!
WELL WHAT I ALWAYS SAY IS THAT YOU CAN'T KEEP A RICH MAN ALL TO YOURSELF WHEN I'M HERE
ANYWAY I THINK WE SIMPLY MUST GET TO THE BALCONY SO THAT SO I CAN PREPARE MYSELF. I'M FEELING LUCKY
DRINK MISS?.. PLEASE?

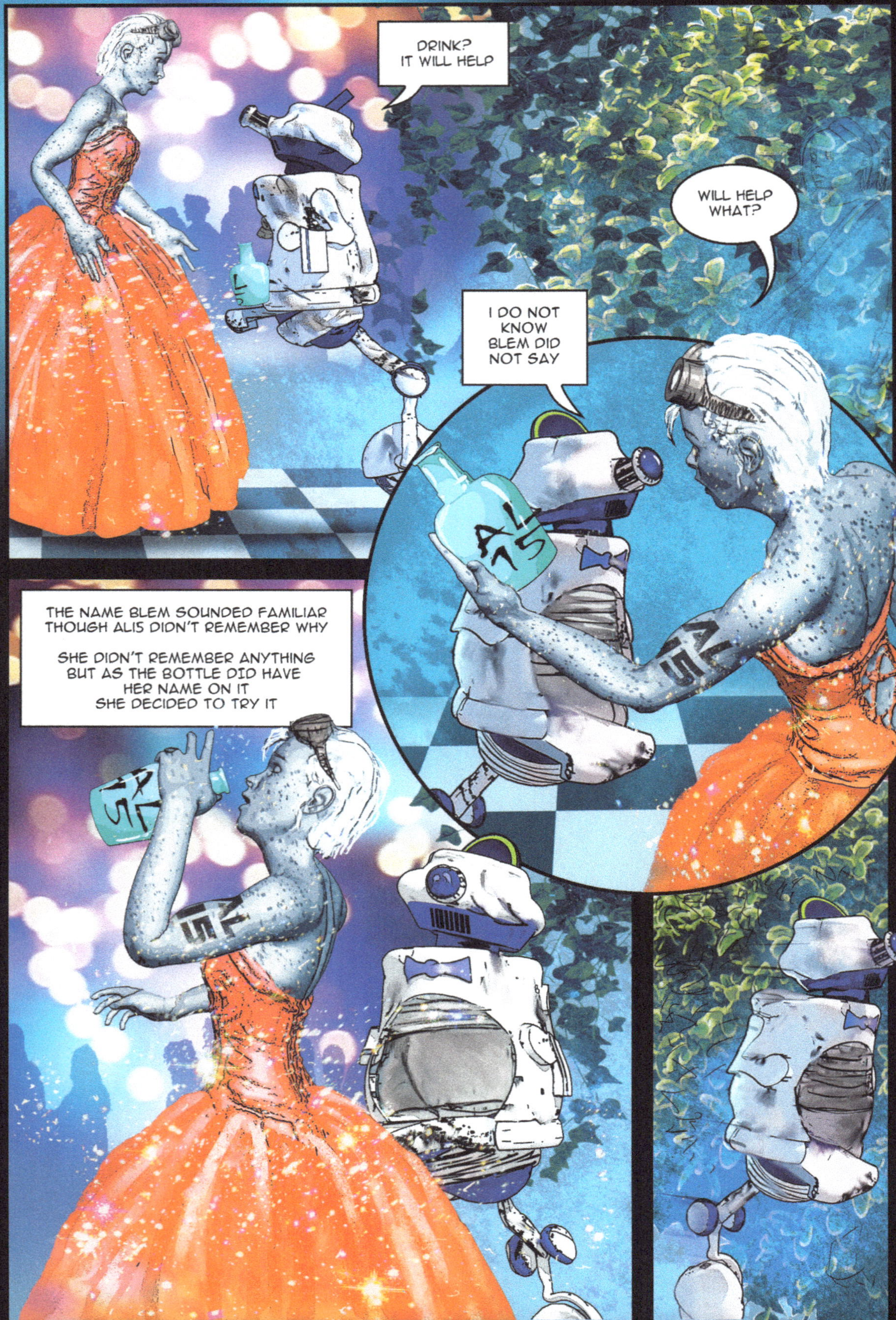
DRINK?
IT WILL HELP
WILL HELP
WHAT?
I DO NOT
KNOW
BLEM DID
NOT SAY
THE NAME BLEM SOUNDED FAMILIAR
THOUGH ALIS DIDN'T REMEMBER WHY
SHE DIDN'T REMEMBER ANYTHING
BUT AS THE BOTTLE DID HAVE
HER NAME ON IT
SHE DECIDED TO TRY IT

TASTES AWFUL SO WHAT DO...
HEY! WAIT
OK SO.. EITHER IT WANTS ME TO FOLLOW IT THROUGH..
..OR.. IT REALLY DOESN'T WANT ME TO FOLLOW IT THROUGH..
I'LL FOLLOW IT THROUGH

WELL THE CPU IS REPAIRED SO IT SHOULD BE WORKING BUT NO MOBILITY FUNCTIONS YET
I'M COMING TOO! & I BROUGHT SOME SAP FOR AL15
AL 15
NO YOU'RE NOT
BLEM IT WILL BE DANGEROUS & BESIDES WHO'S GOING TO LOOK AFTER THE MOON WHEN I'M GONE?
HERE THIS IS FOR YOU
I HAVE IMPORTANT MAYORING TO DO SO YOU HAVE TO GIVE THIS TO AL15. IT WILL HELP
EITHER PUTTING THE BOTTLE ON ITS TRAY OR PATTING IT ON THE HEAD OR GIVING IT AN INSTRUCTION, OR A COMBINATION OF ALL THREE, MADE THE DROID LIGHT UP, WOBBLE & EVENTUALLY STAND
I DIDN'T DO IT
CANAPÉ?.... CANAPÉ?... CANAPÉ?..
YOU'VE ACTIVATED IT! ..OF COURSE YOU CLEVER THING! IT'S A SERVICE DROID IT JUST NEEDED A PURPOSE TO WORK
YES I AM CLEVER. & I KNOW ITS NAME IS CANAPÉ

NO IT'S JUST REBOOTING IT WAS OFFERING YOU A SNACK ..PART OF ITS OLD PROGRAM.. IT DOESN'T HAVE A NAME
THAT THOUGHT SEEMED TO AGITATE THE LITTLE GARDENER GREATLY
YOU CAN'T NOT HAVE A NAME! YOU'D GET LOST! I'D GIVE HIM MINE BUT THEN I WOULDN'T HAVE ONE & I'D GET LOST & THAT WOULD BE VERY SAD
OK OK YOU'RE RIGHT ITS NAME IS CANAPÉ! NOW YOU NEED TO STAND CLEAR SO WE CAN TAKE-OFF
HA I THOUGHT SO
HOW LONG WILL YOU BE?
NOT LONG. BECAUSE WE'LL BE TRAVELLING BACKWARDS WE CAN RETURN ON THEIR NEXT WORMHOLE, MEANING WE COULD THEORETICALLY END UP BACK HERE ONLY A FEW SECONDS AFTER WE LEAVE!
SO I GET TO BE MAYOR FOR JUST A FEW SECONDS?
ERM YES
COOL!

AS AL15 FINDS HER WAY THROUGH THE MAZE THE LEAFY BUSHES DISSOLVE INTO COLD STONE WITH EACH STEP HER MEMORY WAS SLOWLY STARTING TO RETURN
..I'M HERE TO.. FIND.. SOMETHING
..MY HOME..
I'M HERE TO FIND MY HOME
..MY WAY HOME
AL15 IT'S YOU!
HEY DO I KNOW YOU?
LOOK OUT AL15!
I THOUGHT I SAW...
MY CLOTHES... MY DRESS...
SHE CAN'T SEE US
WE ARE LOSING HER!
WHAT IS HAPPENING?
AL15 NOTHING IS WHAT IT SEEMS
PRESS SOME BUTTONS

WHAT THE...?
WHERE AM I?
& MORE IMPORTANTLY
WHY AM I IN THIS STU..WAIT ....WHAT?
I'VE BEEN HERE BEFORE BUT..I CAN'T REM..WHAT.
..I DON'T.. ..I'M...
COOEEE ALIS !

SOMNIUM TERRAM
Gdzie rodzą się sny
SYLWESTER
ZBIÓRKA CHARYTATYWNA
WIDOWISKOWE!
TEJ NOCY
Wszystkie wpływy przeznaczone będą na
fundusz pomocy Viridi
program pomocy Miror
ONI NA TO ZASŁUGUJĄ
Specjalny gość honorowy
GEROME PATRICK IV
CEO Korporacja Patriam
JESTEŚMY DUMNI BĘDĄC CZĘŚCIĄ
KORPORACJA PATRIAM
STWORZONY DLA TWOJEJ PRZYSZŁOŚCI

TU JESTEŚ ! SCHOWANA W OGRODZIE JAK ZAWSZE.
W SAMĄ PORĘ NA FAJERWERKI! TAKI SZCZYTNY CEL: BIEDNE GŁODUJĄCE DZIECI Z VIRIDI
CO? JA JESTEM Z VIRIDI. NIKT TAM NIE GŁODUJE. WYTWARZAMY JEDZENIE.
TAK, OCZYWIŚCIE KOCHANIE TO MIŁO.
ZAREZERWOWAŁAM DLA NAS MIEJSCE NA BALKONIE WARTE KAŻDEJ ZŁOTÓWKI !
PLOTKA GŁOSI , ŻE GEROME PATRICK IV POŁĄCZY SIĘ Z NAMI NA ŻYWO. NIEZŁE CIACHO MOŻLIE, ŻE MAŻ NR 7!
CÓŻ ZAWSZE POWTARZAM, ŻE NIE MOŻESZ ZACHOWAĆ BOGACZA TYKO DL A SIEBIE.
TAK CZY SIAK POWINNYŚMY IŚĆ NA BALKON. MUSZĘ SIĘ PRZYGOTOWAĆ. I'M FEELING LUCKY

SO HOW USEFUL ARE YOU? I MEAN COULD YOU STEER THIS SHIP?
WHY WOULD I KNOW ANYTHING ABOUT SPACESHIPS?
WELL YOU ARE DRESSED IN A.. OH NEVER MIND I KNOW.. 'LONG STORY' ..JUST GO & FIND SOMEWHERE TO SIT
WAIT A MINUTE! WONT WE END UP LIKE THIS THING DID? ALL MANGLED UP?
NO THESE SHIPS ARE DESIGNED AS FARADAY CAGES FOR EMP PROTECTION IT'LL BLOCK ALL ELECTROMAGNETIC FIELDS
THERE MAY BE A FEW ELECTRO-STATIC DISCHARGES THOUGH
GOOD! SO.. WE'RE SAFE THEN?
ISH
JUST .. TRY NOT TO TOUCH ANYTHING METAL

..ONE.. ..TWO.. ..THREE.. ..FOUR..

ALIS WAS ABOUT TO FOLLOW THE EXUBERANT WOMAN
WHEN SOMETHING ABOUT THE MAZE CAUGHT HER EYE
THE MORE SHE LOOKED AT THE HEDGE THE MORE
A SHADOWY SHAPE
STARTED TO APPEAR FROM
THE PATTERN OF THE LEAVES
IS SOMEBODY THERE?
THE SHADOW WAS A SMALL FIGURE SLOWLY MOVING
TOWARDS HER
THERE WAS AN AIR OF CALM ABOUT THE APPARITION
IT BENT DOWN & PICKED UP A FAMILIAR LOOKING BOTTLE
FROM THE FLOOR.
THEN OFFERED IT TO AL15
HOW ARE YOU DOING THAT?
IS THAT FOR ME?
AL15 WAS TRANSFIXED BY THE MOMENT
& GENTLY TOOK THE BOTTLE
FROM THE SHADOW'S OUTSTRETCHED REACH
& POLITELY TOOK A DRINK
ER..THANK YOU ?
OH DO HURRY UP ALIS THE BALCONY AWAITS YOU'LL MISS THE SPEECH!
THE MOMENT WAS GONE
AS WAS THE APPARITION
OK, COMING!.. (WHOEVER YOU ARE)
AL 15
AL 15

10/6
I MAY HAVE TOUCHED SOMETHING METAL

WELL I GUESS THIS IS THE BALCONY

ZUGZWANG MEGALOPOLIS
WELL ALI5 HAS DEFINITELY BEEN HERE!
I HAVE DISABLED THE ALARMS NOW LET'S MAKE A PLAN

GOOD EVENING INSERT.. MADAME WH..
I'M BUSY!
RIGHT, NOW GUEST LIST..
NO NAMES JUST DETAILS
OK.. LAST VISITOR .. HUMAN VIRIDIAN MUST BE HER!
THERE WE ARE REF: 134740 DESIGNATION N.Y.E. 802
CANAPÉ WE NEED TO GET HERE UNNOTICED

ALIS DIDN'T HAVE LONG TO TAKE IN THE VIEW BECAUSE EVERYTHING WENT.. STRANGE
ALIS JUST IN TIME THE SHOW'S STARTED!
WHERE'S THIS COMING FROM?
IT'S PROJECTED FROM THE TOWER SO CLEVER!
OBVIOUSLY GEROME NEVER LEAVES THE TOWER PERSONALLY
I'M HOPING FOR AN INVITE ONE DAY I DO CONTRIBUTE HEAVILY TO HIS CHARITIES
OO THREE MINUTES LEFT HOW EXCITING
LEFT FOR WHAT?
NEW YEARS SILLY NOW SHUSH HERE HE COMES!
GEROME! GEROME! COOEE GEROME!

11:57
Gerome Patrick IV
VIRIDI RELIEF FUND
GEROME PATRICK IV
LIVE
00:02:28
PLEDGED
738,957,267.37

LEVEL 05
WHAT?
LEVEL 06
I SAID JUMP OUT AT LEVEL 8!
LEVEL 07

HURRY UP!
SERVICE DROIDS
HIDE!
LEVEL 08
WJ807
AL 15
LEVEL 08

WILD JUNGLE
GOOD EVENING SIR, YOU APPEAR TO BE IN THE WRONG PLACE I WILL CALL FOR ASSIST
NO NEED
WILL YOU STOP SHOOTING THINGS?!
YES WHEN YOU REALIZE PUTTING YOUR LIGHTS OUT ISN'T HIDING!!

THIS WILL HELP
IT'LL BE FINE CANAPE I ONLY WOUNDED IT
WAIT A MINUTE THE BULLET HOLE!
IT'S.. THE SAME ONE!

OF COURSE!! IT MAKES SENSE NOW
THEY ARE THE SAME DROID!
RIGHT I NEED TO TAKE OUT THE PROTOCOL CHIP TO MAKE IT SAFE...
DON'T YOU SEE? AL15 WOULDN'T HAVE KNOWN HOW TO ADD THOSE MESSAGES. & SHE DOESN'T CALL ME CASSY. SHE DIDN'T SEND THE DROID THROUGH THE WORMHOLE TO GET ME.. I DID! THAT'S HOW IT KNEW MY NAME
HMM THEY DO LOOK VERY SIMILAR
BUT YOU THINK YOU'D REMEMBER SOMETHING LIKE THAT?
NO THAT'S BECAUSE IT HASN'T HAPPENED YET
BUT IT'S ABOUT TO
YOU TWO WAIT HERE & STAY OUT OF TROUBLE
COME ON FUTURE CANAPE
YOU'VE GOT A WORMHOLE TO CATCH!

OK BYE! WE'LL JUST WAIT HERE
WELL THAT MADE NO SENSE! LUCKY I'M HERE TO KEEP THIS GROUP ON MISSION
DON'T WORRY LITTLE ONE I'M SURE YOU'LL BE ABLE TO HELP TOO
AL
LOOK OUT THOSE DROIDS ARE ON THEIR WAY BACK!
REMEMBER TO KEEP HIDDEN CANAPÉ
CANAPÉ?
AL 15

NOW I NEED YOU TO GO TOWARDS THE WORMHOLE & DON'T STOP
I'M CASSY GO FIND ME
OH AND... SORRY ABOUT THE LANDING

THE DROID TRUMBLED TOWARDS THE EYE OF THE STORM AS INSTRUCTED LIGHTNING FORKS STRETCHED TOWARDS THE METAL OBJECT AND SCOOPED IT UP SUCKING IT INTO THE VOID
THE WORMHOLE COLLAPSED ITSELF AROUND THE DROID PERMENANTLY CLOSING THE SPACE RUPTURE BEHIND IT
IT SEEMED ALMOST AS IF THE WORMHOLE KNEW THAT ITS PURPOSE WAS COMPLETE
MEANWHILE
CANAPÉ! WHERE HAVE YOU BEEN? I'VE BEEN OUT OF MY MIND WITH WORRY
NYE802
I SERVED AL15 THE DRINK IT HELPED LOOK

NEW YEA
NYE802
AL15 IT'S YOU!
HEY DO I KNOW YOU?
LOOK OUT AL15!
AL15!
SHE CAN'T SEE US
I THOUGHT I SAW...
AL 15
E802
MY CLOTHES... MY DRESS

WHAT IS HAPPENING?
ALIS NOTHING IS WHAT IT SEEMS!

NEW YEARS
NYE802
DEEP OCEAN
WHAT IS HAPPENING?
ALI5 NOTHING IS WHAT IT SEEMS!
WE ARE LOSING HER!
CANAPÉ PRESS SOME BUTTONS
IT'S OK KEEP GOING! I GOT THIS
WOAH I DON'T GOT THIS

DEEP OCEAN
DON'T MIND ME SHOOTING THEM NOW DO YA?
WILD JUNGLE

SO CLOSE
IT WAS HARD FOR MARCUS TO TELL CASSIOPEIA THAT THEY SAW HER DAUGHTER BUT WERE UNABLE TO DO ANYTHING ABOUT IT.
IT WAS HARD FOR CASSIOPEIA TO REASSURE MARCUS THAT HE HAD DONE ALL HE COULD THOUGH SHE REALIZED SHE NEEDED TO
IT WAS ALSO HARD FOR CANAPE TO UNDERSTAND WHY THE DRINK HADN'T HELPED MORE
TOGETHER THEY PICKED THEMSELVES UP
SHE WAS RIGHT THERE! BEHIND THOSE LASERS BUT THOSE THINGS TOOK HER BACK!
IT'S OK TELL ME WHAT HAPPENED
HE TOLD HER HOW AL15 LOOKED CONFUSED APPEARING TO ALMOST BUT NOT QUITE NOTICE THEM
HOW SHE HAD SOMETHING ON THE SIDE OF HER HEAD. A SMALL GLOWING DISK
CASSY AT ONCE RECOGNIZED WHAT IT WAS
A TVI! TEMPLE VISION IMPLANT THEY WERE USED FOR AUGMENTED REALITY META WORLDS BUT THEY WERE BANNED YEARS AGO!
SHE WAS ALSO SHOWN THE BUTTONS THEY PRESSED
HOLD ON, DID YOU PRESS THIS RESET BUTTON?
CANAPE PRESSED THEM ALL, WHY?
IT HAS CHANGED THE LANGUAGE! SHE'S NOW SPEAKING... POLISH? ONE OF THE OLD EARTH LANGUAGES...THAT WILL JUST CONFUSE HER THERE.. RESET
ONE OF THEIR LANGUAGES?
YES THEY USED TO HAVE DIFFERENT ONES BACK THEN IT KEPT EARTH PEOPLE SEPARATE
DOESN'T SOUND VERY FRIENDLY
THAT'S HISTORY, BUT IT ALL WORKED OUT IN THE END.. PATRIAM SAVED US FROM ALL OF THAT NONSENSE.
ERM.. NOT SURE THAT'S EXACTLY WHAT HAPPENED WELL NOT ACCORDING TO AL15 ANYWAY

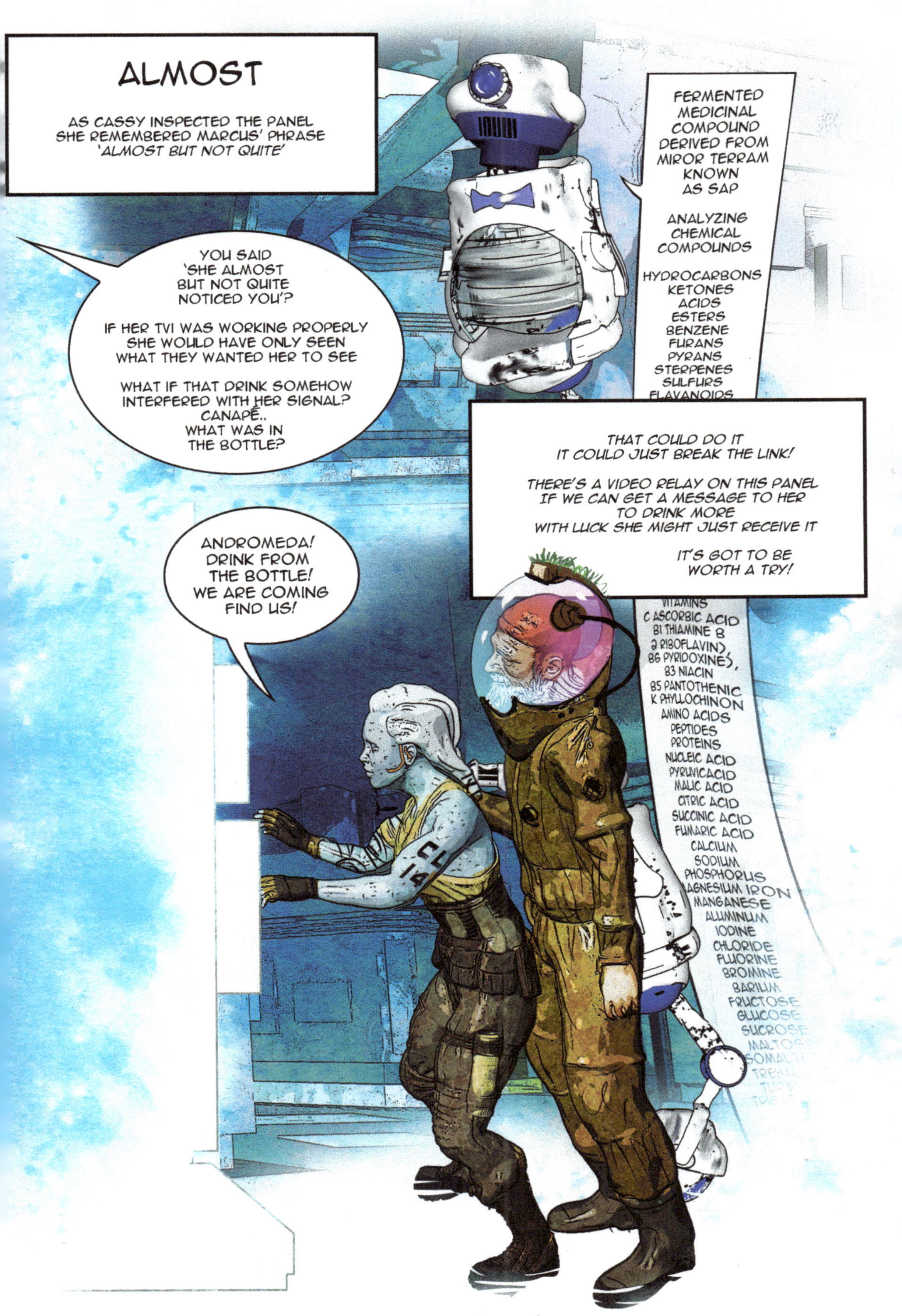
ALMOST
AS CASSY INSPECTED THE PANEL SHE REMEMBERED MARCUS' PHRASE 'ALMOST BUT NOT QUITE'
FERMENTED MEDICINAL COMPOUND DERIVED FROM MIROR TERRAM KNOWN AS SAP
ANALYZING CHEMICAL COMPOUNDS
HYDROCARBONS KETONES ACIDS ESTERS BENZENE FURANS PYRANS STERPENES SULFURS
YOU SAID 'SHE ALMOST BUT NOT QUITE NOTICED YOU'?
IF HER TVI WAS WORKING PROPERLY SHE WOULD HAVE ONLY SEEN WHAT THEY WANTED HER TO SEE
WHAT IF THAT DRINK SOMEHOW INTERFERED WITH HER SIGNAL? CANAPÉ.. WHAT WAS IN THE BOTTLE?
THAT COULD DO IT IT COULD JUST BREAK THE LINK!
THERE'S A VIDEO RELAY ON THIS PANEL IF WE CAN GET A MESSAGE TO HER TO DRINK MORE WITH LUCK SHE MIGHT JUST RECEIVE IT
IT'S GOT TO BE WORTH A TRY!
ANDROMEDA! DRINK FROM THE BOTTLE! WE ARE COMING FIND US!
C ASCORBIC ACID
B1 THIAMINE B
2 RIBOFLAVIN
B6 PYRIDOXINE
B3 NIACIN
B5 PANTOTHENIC
K PHYLLOCHINON
AMINO ACIDS
PEPTIDES
PROTEINS
NUCLEIC ACID
PYRUVICACID
MALIC ACID
CITRIC ACID
SUCCINIC ACID
FUMARIC ACID
CALCIUM
SODIUM
PHOSPHORUS
IRON
MANGANESE
ALUMINUM
IODINE
CHLORIDE
FLUORINE
BROMINE
BARIUM
FRUCTOSE
GLUCOSE
SUCROSE

FRIENDS YOUR GENEROSITY ONCE AGAIN OVERWHELMS ME DONATIONS ARE GATHERING APACE. IT LOOKS AS THOUGH..
11:57
GEROME PATRICK IV
LIVE
OFFICIAL COUNT
00:02:28
TONITE'S PLEDGED
958,957,267,972
......GOT TO BE WORTH A TRY
11:57
ANDROMEDA! DRINK FROM THE BOTTLE WE ARE COMING FIND US!
MOM?
... YOUR TIPS TO A PARTICIPATING DROID NEAR YOU & LET'S END HUNGER ON VIRIDI ONCE & FOR ALL! THEY DESERVE IT!
11:58
DID YOU SEE THAT?
GEROME PATRICK IV
YES I TOLD YOU HE WAS DISHY!

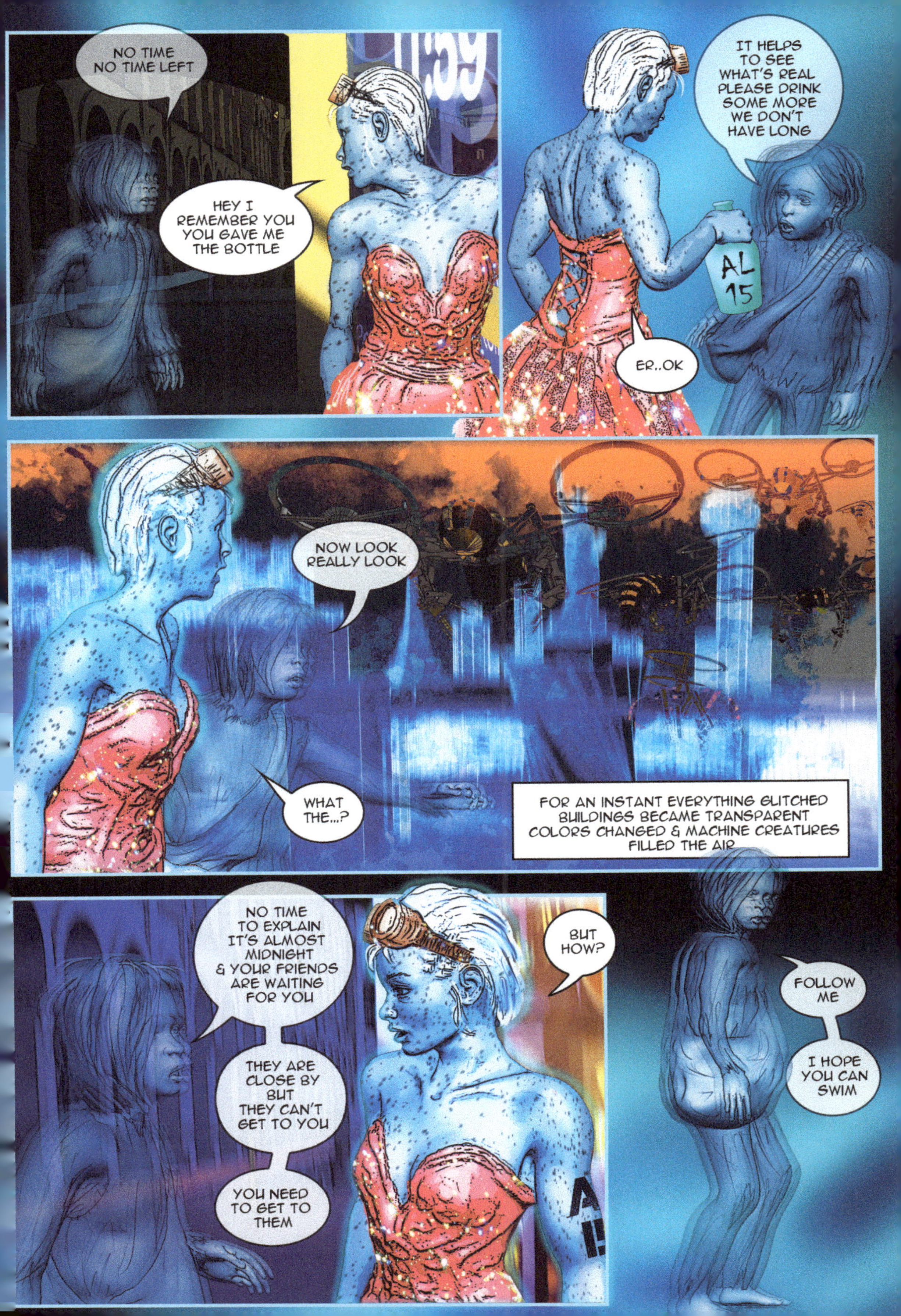
NO TIME
NO TIME LEFT
HEY I REMEMBER YOU YOU GAVE ME THE BOTTLE
IT HELPS TO SEE WHAT'S REAL PLEASE DRINK SOME MORE WE DON'T HAVE LONG
AL 15
ER..OK
NOW LOOK REALLY LOOK
WHAT THE...?
FOR AN INSTANT EVERYTHING GLITCHED BUILDINGS BECAME TRANSPARENT COLORS CHANGED & MACHINE CREATURES FILLED THE AIR
NO TIME TO EXPLAIN IT'S ALMOST MIDNIGHT & YOUR FRIENDS ARE WAITING FOR YOU
BUT HOW?
THEY ARE CLOSE BY BUT THEY CAN'T GET TO YOU
YOU NEED TO GET TO THEM
FOLLOW ME
I HOPE YOU CAN SWIM

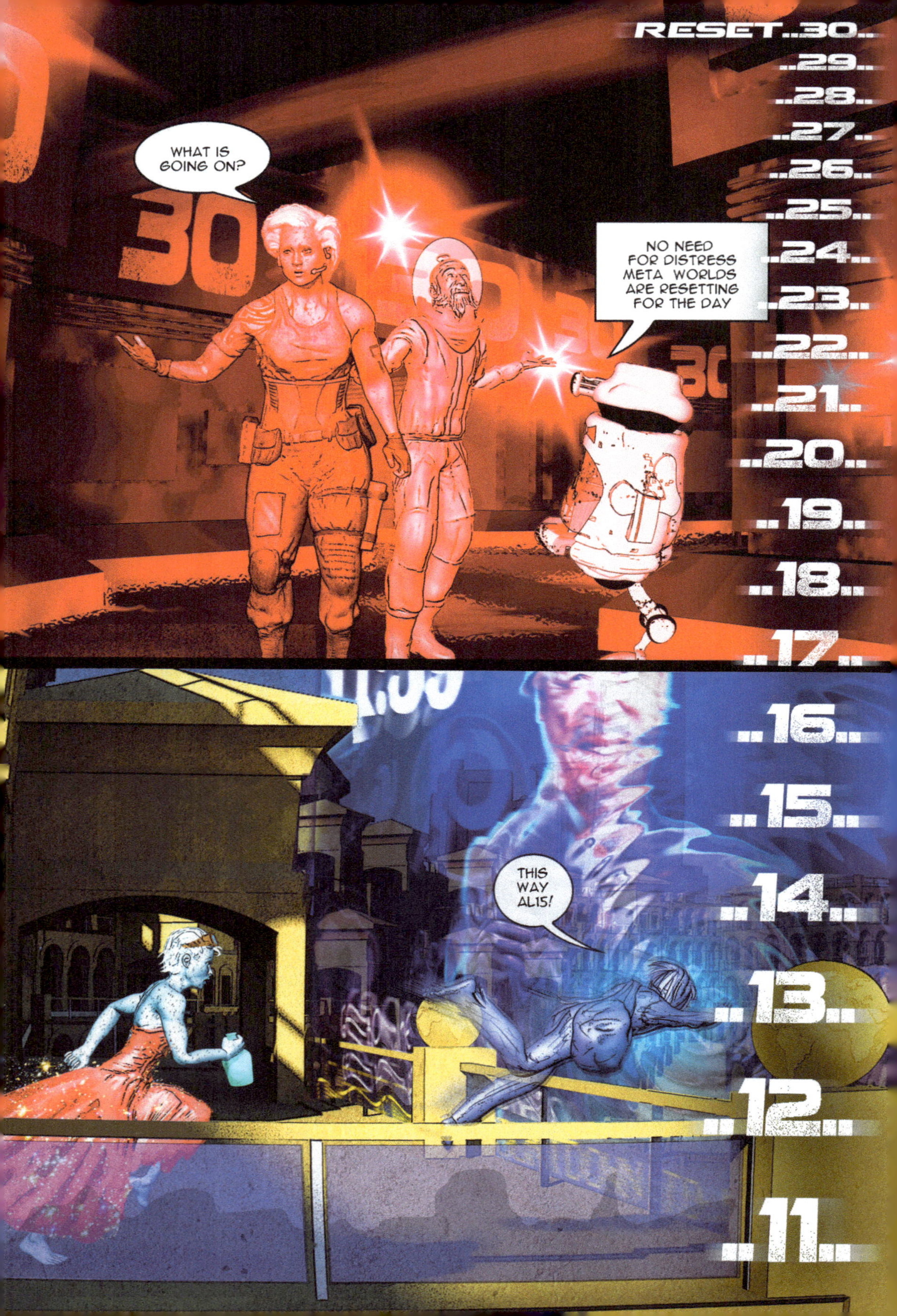
RESET..30..
..29..
..28..
..27..
..26..
..25..
WHAT IS GOING ON?
NO NEED FOR DISTRESS META WORLDS ARE RESETTING FOR THE DAY
..24..
..23..
..22..
..21..
..20..
..19..
..18..
..17..
..16..
..15..
THIS WAY AL15!
..14..
..13..
..12..
..11..

LEAP OF FAITH

09

THE CROWD HAD STARTED TO COUNT DOWN TO MIDNIGHT REMINDING ALIS JUST HOW LITTLE TIME SHE HAD LEFT

08

JUMPING OFF OF A HIGH BALCONY DIDN'T SEEM LIKE THE MOST SENSIBLE IDEA

07

BUT THEN...

06

NOTHING ABOUT THIS WORLD DID

05

WHAT ALIS DID KNOW WAS THAT SHE DID NOT BELONG HERE

04

THE WOMAN SEEMED TO KNOW HER.. BUT

03

THE SHADOW FIGURE'S WORDS RANG THE MOST TRUE

02

AND ALIS FELT HER MOTHER WAS LOOKING FOR HER

01

NO TIME LEFT

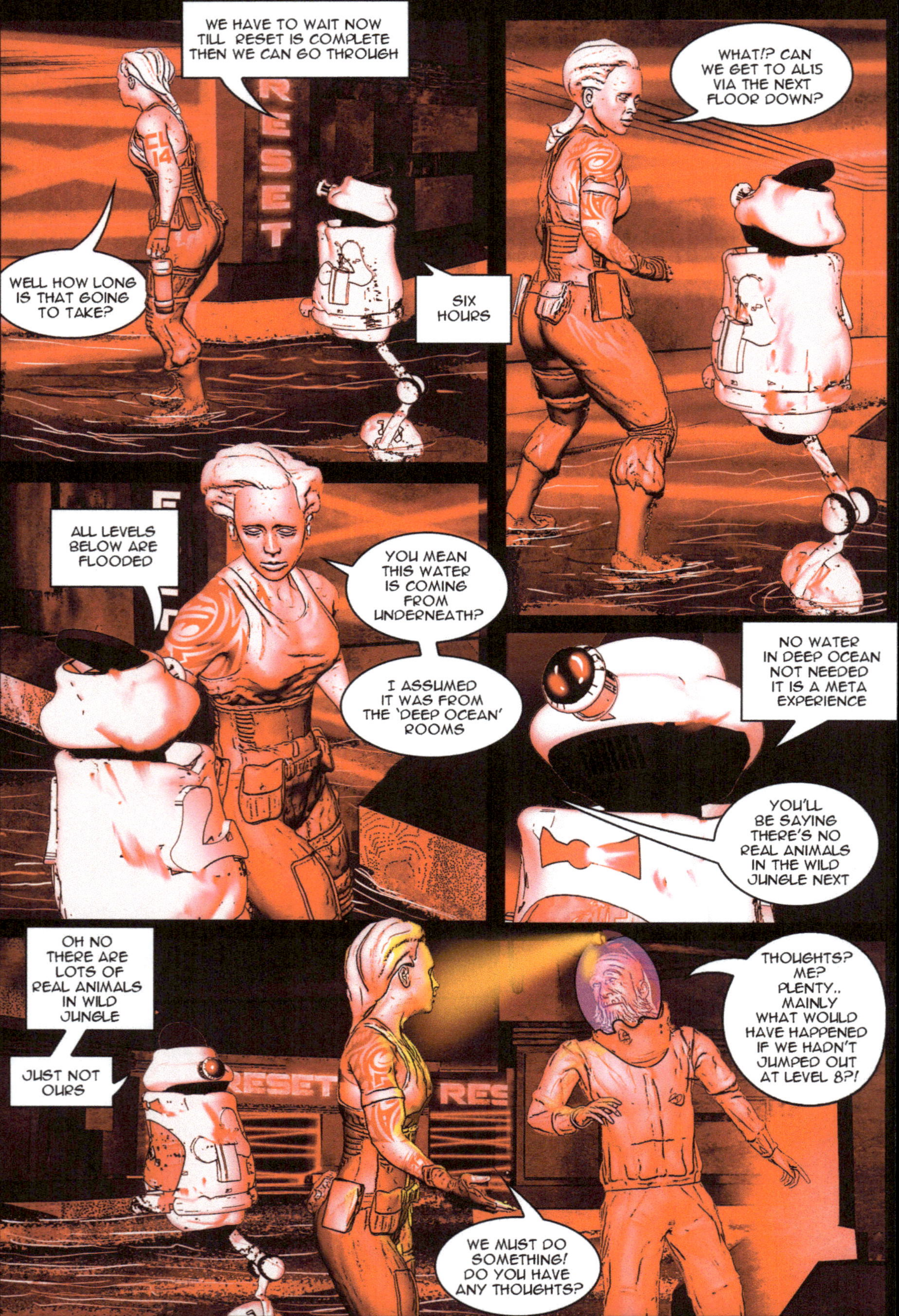
WE HAVE TO WAIT NOW TILL RESET IS COMPLETE THEN WE CAN GO THROUGH
RESET
WELL HOW LONG IS THAT GOING TO TAKE?
SIX HOURS
WHAT!? CAN WE GET TO AL15 VIA THE NEXT FLOOR DOWN?
ALL LEVELS BELOW ARE FLOODED
YOU MEAN THIS WATER IS COMING FROM UNDERNEATH?
I ASSUMED IT WAS FROM THE 'DEEP OCEAN' ROOMS
NO WATER IN DEEP OCEAN NOT NEEDED IT IS A META EXPERIENCE
YOU'LL BE SAYING THERE'S NO REAL ANIMALS IN THE WILD JUNGLE NEXT
OH NO THERE ARE LOTS OF REAL ANIMALS IN WILD JUNGLE
JUST NOT OURS
RESET
RES
WE MUST DO SOMETHING! DO YOU HAVE ANY THOUGHTS?
THOUGHTS? ME? PLENTY.. MAINLY WHAT WOULD HAVE HAPPENED IF WE HADN'T JUMPED OUT AT LEVEL 8?!

THE MACHINES HADN'T NOTICED HER & AL15 WAS CAREFUL TO KEEP IT THAT WAY
EVERYWHERE SHE LOOKED, PEOPLE WERE BEING SHEPHERDED AWAY BY THESE DRONES

THE SHADOWY FIGURE HAD SWAM TOWARDS A RAFT & WAS HELPED ABOARD BY OTHERS SIMILAR

THEY BECKONED AL15 TOWARDS THEM

HURRY! OVER HERE
QUICK BEFORE THEY PICK UP YOUR SCENT!
I'M NOT COMING ANY CLOSER TILL I FIND OUT WHAT IS GOING ON..
AND WHO YOU ARE..
AND WHAT ON VIRIDI IS THIS THING ON THE SIDE OF MY HEAD?!
BESIDES THOSE MACHINES HAVEN'T NOTICED ME SO FAR

ITS NOT THE MACHINES WE'RE TALKING ABOUT!

SHE'S BEEN DOWN THERE TOO LONG NOW
I SAID IT WAS TOO DANGEROUS
NO.. WAIT LOOK!
WE'VE LOST HER
LOOK OUT!

WELL ARE YOU GONNA HELP ME UP THEN?

IS IT
JUST ME?
OR IS
THIS WATER
GETING
DEEPER?
YOU
THINK?!
RESET

THANK YOU
ARE YOU.. GHOSTS?
HA NO, WE ARE JUST AS REAL AS YOU
WE REALIZE YOU HAVE LOTS OF QUESTIONS. THEY ALL DO BUT YOU DON'T HAVE TIME FOR US TO EXPLAIN
YOU'LL SOON BE OUT OF HERE JUST FORGET ABOUT US
WELL THAT'S NOT GOING TO HAPPEN!
I WANT TO KNOW I WANT TO UNDERSTAND
WHAT IS THIS PLACE? & WHAT HAPPENED HERE?

THIS PLACE? THIS PLACE WAS ONCE A UTOPIA! A HAVEN FOR THE RICH
OVER THE SPAN OF YEARS THE GUESTS SPENT MORE & MORE MONEY & TIME USING THE METAVERSES & LESS TIME IN THE REALITY OF THEIR OWN LIVES.
AS THE GARDENS & BUILDINGS GOT INTO DISREPAIR NO-ONE SEEMED TO CARE THE AUGMENTED REALITY HAD ALL THEY NEEDED AND WANTED
IN FACT THE MORE DATA THE SYSTEM COLLECTED FROM THEM, THE MORE THE SYSTEM SHOWED THEM WHAT THEY WANTED TO SEE SO PEOPLE STAYED IN THEIR 'IDEAL' WORLDS AND WERE VERY HAPPY TO PAY FOR THINGS THEY'LL NEVER HAVE
THE PATRIAM SYSTEM DEVELOPED TO MEET THEIR NEEDS IS JUST A BUNCH OF ALGORITHMS. IT HAS NO FEELINGS IT CALCULATED THAT AUGMENTED REALITY WAS ALL THE GUESTS NEEDED TO KEEP THE MONEY FLOWING
THEIR MEMORIES ARE THEN WIPED & THE DAY IS REPEATED OVER AND OVER AGAIN
THOSE FIREWORKS WERE YOUR RESET LIGHTS
THEY EVEN GET THOSE POOR PEOPLE COUNTING DOWN!
WE WERE ONCE PART OF THIS SYSTEM
BUT HAVE BECOME DISCONNECTED

THERE ARE
MANY OF US

WE LIVE IN THE DESERTED BUILDINGS ABOVE GROUND

RADIATION FROM THE WORMHOLES HAS AFFECTED US

PROLONGED EXPOSURE HAS PUT US SLIGHTLY OUT OF TIME

WE ARE BOTH HERE AND A SPLIT SECOND IN THE PAST
WHICH IS WHY WE APPEAR AS WE DO

THIS TRAIT HAS BEEN OUR GREATEST ALLY
AS THE MACHINES CANNOT DETECT US

WE TAKE IT IN TURNS TO WATCH OVER EVERYONE
RESCUING WHOEVER WE CAN
WHOEVER BECOMES DISCONNECTED

MOST OF THE TIME WE ARE HELPLESS
APART FROM JUST BEING OBSERVERS

WE SAW YOU WHEN YOU FIRST ARRIVED

FOR YOUR SAKE WE HAD HOPED THE DRAGONS WOULD SCARE YOU OFF
BUT YOU ARE OBVIOUSLY MADE OF STERNER STUFF!

SO THAT'S WHAT THIS DOES!
OUCH!
YOU NEED TO WAIT IT WILL RELEASE ITSELF SOON
SO HOW DID YOU GUYS GET 'DISCONNECTED'?
FOR SOME THE IMPLANTS JUST FAILED OR THE DATA WAS CORRUPTED
FOR OTHERS THEIR MONEY GETS DRAINED & THEIR CONNECTIONS SIMPLY STOP
I WATCH MY FAMILY EVERY DAY I HOPE THAT I CAN SAVE AT LEAST ONE OF THEM BEFORE IT'S TOO LATE
WHAT DO YOU MEAN? TOO LATE?
ALL THE FLOORS BELOW US ARE FLOODED. THIS ONE IS NEXT
AL 15
WHOEVER DECIDED TO BUILD THIS CITY MOSTLY UNDERGROUND DID NOT UNDERSTAND THIS LAND'S ECO-SYSTEM
THE ROCK HERE IS POROUS. IT WAS NEVER MADE TO BE DUG INTO, RESHAPED OR FORM WALLS. IT HOLDS THE WATER WHEN THE RAINS COME
THIS SEASON WILL BE THE LAST FOR LEVEL 8

WHAT ABOUT ALL THE PEOPLE? WE CANT JUST LEAVE THEM HERE!?
WE HAVE NO CHOICE WHILST THEY ARE CONNECTED THE MACHINES WONT ALLOW THEM TO LEAVE
SURELY I CAN HELP IN SOME WAY
WHY DON'T YOU GET THAT GEROME PERSON TO LET THEM GO?
WHO?
YOU KNOW.. GEROME SOMEBODY. CEO OF PATRIAM?
YOU MEAN THE VIDEO? THAT HAS BEEN TRANSMITTING WAY BEFORE ANY OF US WERE HERE
I DOUBT THAT HE EVER EXISTED AND IF HE DID IT WAS A VERY LONG TIME AGO!
AL 15
I KNOW YOU WANT TO HELP & WE THANK YOU
BUT THERE'S NOTHING YOU CAN DO. YOU'RE JUST ONE PERSON
BUT YOU, WE CAN HELP YOU DO NOT DESERVE OUR FATE.
OK FIRSTLY YOU DO NOT DESERVE YOUR FATE
& SECONDLY ONE PERSON CAN DO A LOT!
BESIDES I'VE GOT MY MOM BACKING ME UP
NOW WHERE ARE THEY?

THEY ARE IN THE CORRIDORS WAITING FOR YOU
YOU CAN GET TO THEM BY GOING THROUGH THE META MOUNTAINS
THEN GO BACK TO YOUR HOME & BE SAFE
BUT I CAN BE OF HELP HERE
NO, PROMISE YOU'LL TAKE THEM TO SAFETY?
PLEASE?
OK, I PROMISE
THE WAY TO GET TO THE SURFACE UNNOTICED IS VIA THE WILD JUNGLE
IT COLLAPSED A LONG TIME AGO & IS NO LONGER USED IT IS POSSIBLE TO CLIMB OUT FROM THERE.
IN EFFECT IT ACTUALLY HAS BECOME A WILD JUNGLE
BE WARY THOUGH FOR PEOPLE WHO HAVEN'T BECOME TIME-PHASED, IT CAN BE A VERY HAZARDOUS PLACE
THE INDIGENOUS ANIMALS HAVE TAKEN OVER THE WHOLE AREA
IN THAT CASE.. CAN I BORROW SOME OF YOUR BAIT? I MIGHT NEED A PEACE OFFERING

THE META ROOMS HAD FINISHED RESETTING AND FOR THE GUESTS OF LEVEL 8 LIFE WAS CONTINUING AS NORMAL.
YET ANOTHER NEW DAY OF THE SAME DAY
COOEE ALIS WHERE ARE YOU? HIDING IN THE GARDEN AS USUAL?
I WANTED YOUR OPINION ON THIS DRESS FOR TONITE
IS THE FUR TOO MUCH? IT'S FAUX MAMMOTH
ALIS?
ALIS? ARE YOU IN THAT MAZE?
WELL I'M NOT COMING IN THERE TO FIND YOU
NOT IN THESE HEELS!
I'VE PUT IN A BID FOR A PLACE ON THE BALCONY TONITE FOR BOTH OF US
I'M FEELING LUCKY!
SO DON'T BE LATE NOW
DRINK BOT, YOU'LL HAVE TO DO! FOLLOW ME TO THE JEWELLERS
& I SAW A GORGEOUS GOLD DRESS EARLIER

WE NEED TO GET TO THE TEMPLE BEFORE WE FREEZE TO DEATH..& PRAY THAT RESCUE COMES IN TIME!
I.. DON'T THINK I CAN.. MAKE IT! CUT THE ROPE SAVE YOURSELF!

EXIT
NOOO! I'LL BE DAMNED IF I LEAVE YOU BEHIND WE'VE COME SO FAR WE CAN MAKE IT TOGETHER!
NO TIME! IT'S GIVING WAY!!
AVALANCHE ADVENTURE
TIME REMAINING 03:28:00
OH OK.. I EXPECTED THIS ROOM TO BE BIGGER

RIGHT IT'S CLEAR. WHEN WE GO IN WE'LL GO IN FAST!
THEN SPREAD OUT FIND ANDROMEDA & GET HER OUT
DON'T STOP TILL YOU REACH THE SHIP
WE CAN DO THIS! WE CAN FIND HER!
IF YOU GET INTO TROUBLE USE THIS DRONE SMOKE CANISTER IT WILL CONFUSE THEM GIVING YOU A BETTER CHANCE TO ESCAPE
REMEMBER KEEP IN TOUCH VIA YOUR INTERCOMS
NYE802
NYE802
I DON'T HAVE AN INTERCOM
YES YOU DO. BUTTON ON THE LEFT OF YOUR HELMET
OH I WONDERED WHAT THAT DID

NEW YEARS
NYE802
NYE802
I WOULDN'T GO IN THERE IF I WERE YOU IT'S A RUBBISH PARTY!
NEW YEARS

I THOUGHT I'D LOST YOU!
ERM.. WHERE ARE YOUR BOOTS?

SERIOUSLY? THAT'S YOUR COMMENT?
NOT 'WELL DONE FOR ESCAPING AL15'
'IT MUST HAVE BEEN DANGEROUS AL15'
'WHAT IS THAT GIANT SCARY FISH HEAD AL15?'
BUT.. 'WHERE ARE YOUR BOOTS?'!
AL 15
WELL YOUR FATHER GAVE YOU THOSE BOOTS
ABOUT THE ONLY THING HE DID GIVE ME!
NOW THAT'S NOT FAIR ANDROMEDA! YOU KNOW THAT HE..
ER FOLKS PERHAPS WE COULD CARRY ON THE FAMILY REUNION AFTER WE ESCAPE?

WE CAN CLIMB OUT THROUGH THE JUNGLE
OVER HERE
WILD JUNGLE
NOT IN USE
NOT IN USE
NOT IN USE
NOT POSSIBLE. THIS AREA NOT DESIGNATED IN USE
NOT IN USE
WILD JUNGLE
IT IS NOW. C'MON
I'M CANAPÉ I FOUND YOU I AM USEFUL MAY I CARRY THAT FOR YOU?
ERM YEH SURE THANKS
NOT IN USE
IN USE

FEELING CONFLICTED ABOUT LEAVING
AL15 TOLD CASSY ABOUT ALL THE GUESTS WHO WERE TRAPPED
AND THE DISCONNECTED ONES WHO WEREN'T
SHE TOLD OF THE FATE THAT AWAITS LEVEL 8 WHEN THE RAINS COME
BUT OF THE PROMISE SHE HAD TO MAKE TO GET TO SAFETY
THERE MUST BE SOMETHING WE CAN DO TO HELP THEM?

LET'S REGROUP AT THE SHIP FIRST & GET YOU OUT OF THOSE RAGS
BESIDES WE HAVE TILL THE NEXT WORMHOLE ARRIVES
WOAH IF WE MAKE IT BY THEN!
FOR THE SAKE OF THE MISSION
AL15 IGNORED THE RAGS COMMENT

WILD
JUNGLE

BENEATH THE CANOPY OF WEBS
AL15, CASSY, MARCUS & CANAPÉ
ENTERED A REALM LIKE NO OTHER
TRAPPED MOISTURE HAD CREATED AN EERILY CALM
MARSH-LIKE ENVIRONMENT WITH EVERY SURFACE
SHROUDED IN GOSSAMER VEILS
SOUND DID NOT SEEM TO
PENETRATE THIS HUMID SPACE
BUT ECHOED QUIETLY, ADDING
TO A DISCONCERTINGLY
MUFFLED REVERB
A THOUSAND EYES
SEEMINGLY WATCHING
AS THE ADVENTURERS CAREFULLY STEPPED TOWARDS THE DISTANT GLOW OF FREEDOM
AN OCCASIONAL SMALL ANIMAL FLITTED ACROSS THEIR PATH
LARGE GRAZERS
SHYLY SANK
BACK DOWN
INTO THE BOGS
UNSURE OF THEIR
NEW VISITORS

OH
HEY THERE
LITTLE THING
PUT IT DOWN
WE'VE GOT
ENOUGH
STRAYS
I THINK SHE'S
TALKING
ABOUT US!
SHE WASN'T
BUT CASSY DIDN'T CORRECT THEM
BACK HOME, AL15 HAD, OVER THE YEARS, COLLECTED
A VERITABLE MENAGERIE OF LOST CREATURES
FROM CATS & DIZARDS TO MOON RABBITS & TOVES
YES YOU
LOT GO UP
FIRST..
..I'LL KEEP
AN EYE OUT
DOWN HERE
HOPE YOU
DON'T COME ACROSS
ANY OF THE DAMNED
SPIDERS THAT
MADE THESE
WEBS!
(A TOVE IS LIKE A CROSS BETWEEN
A BADGER & A LIZARD WITH A CURLY TAIL)

WELL THE GOOD NEWS IS..
THEY AREN'T SPIDERS
KEEP STILL! DON'T MOVE
AL 15

I.. DON'T THINK THIS IS WORKING?
JUST KEEP STILL
YOU WANNA TRY IT?
FAIR POINT
HEY! LEAVE MY DAUGHTER ALONE
PLEASE
OH I REALLY DIDN'T WANT TO HAVE TO DO THAT!
SERIOUSLY? YOU DIDN'T WANT TO SHOOT SOMETHING?
NO, IT'S RELEASING PHEROMONES
OTHERS WILL BE ON THEIR WAY
WE NEED TO HURRY
HAVE YOU LOOKED BEHIND YOU? I THINK THEY GOT THE MESSAGE

PHEW I'M GLAD THAT'S OVER!
WHAT ARE YOU LOT LOOKING AT?
WHAT ARE WE GONNA DO?
I DON'T KNOW
WHAT D'YOU MEAN, YOU DON'T KNOW?
TOO MANY TO SHOOT
WE NEED TO GET TO THE OTHER SIDE
WE NEED A DISTRACTION

CANAPÉ KNEW WHAT IT HAD TO DO: A DISTRACTION THEY NEEDED, A DISTRACTION THEY WERE GOING TO GET
MAY I OFFER YOU A FISH CANAPÉ?
THIS WAY PLEASE
OH MY
CANAPÉ RACED AWAY FROM THE OTHERS AS FAST AS ITS WHEEL COULD GO UNTIL IT COULD GO NO FURTHER BUT IT WASN'T FAR OR FAST ENOUGH
AS THE BRAVE LITTLE DROID TURNED TO FACE ITS AGGRESSORS THEY ATTACKED
WITH CANAPE AT THE CORE THE WHOLE NEST SHUDDERED AS ONE

CANAPÉ'S BLINDING SHOCKWAVE HAD SENT THE INSECTS SCAMPERING IN ALL DIRECTIONS
THE PATH IS CLEAR YOU MUST GO NOW THEY WILL BE BACK SOON
THAT WAS AMAZING! C'MON LETS GO!
THE ACT OF BRAVERY HAD COME AT A COST
CANAPÉ?
EIGHT PERCENT
SORRY I AM UNABLE TO CONTINUE WITH YOU
SIX PERCENT
..I .. ..I...... THANK.. YOU.
YOU'RE NOT MAKING SENSE CANAPÉ THANK YOU FOR WHAT?
..MY NAME
PATRIAM REGRETS THE MALFUNCTION OF THIS UNIT 300 CREDITS WILL BE ADDED TO YOUR ACCOUNT FOR ANY AND ALL INCONVENIENCE CAUSED YOU DESERVE IT
WE NEED TO GO

IT WOULDN'T BE RIGHT TO GO YET
HE STILL HAS A LIGHT FLICKERING
WE HAVE TO WAIT
STAND BACK
LET ME HAVE A LOOK
OH I SEE THE PROBLEM
WHAT? NOOO! YOU CAN'T SHOOT CANAPÉ!
AGAIN

RELAX
I'M JUST
SENDING IT
AN INDUCTIVE
CHARGE

YOUR PERSONAL
SERVICE UNIT
IS NOW FULLY
CHARGED AND
READY TO SERVE
YOU DESERVE IT
900 CREDITS
WILL BE DEBITED
FROM YOUR ACCOUN
NOW
CAN WE
GO?

AT THE FOOT OF THE EXIT THE WEARY TRAVELLERS THOUGHT THEY HAD MADE IT
UNTIL THE HEAVENS OPENED
OH NO! THE RAINS HAVE ALREADY STARTED!
IT'S JUST ONE BIG WATERFALL!
WE CAN NOT CLIMB TO THE SURFACE NOW
WE DON'T NEED TO
I'LL CALL THE SHIP
HERMES... CARGO PICKUP THIS SIGNAL'S COORDINATES URGENT

NOW YOU GO UP FIRST & SEND THE LINE BACK DOWN AS SOON AS YOU CAN
DON'T WORRY YOU'LL BE FINE
ACTUALLY THIS FEELS SUPRISINGLY FAMILIAR
AT LEAST I'M NOT BEING HIT WITH A STICK THIS TIME!
WHAT IS HE ON ABOUT?
..NO IDEA

OK ANDROMEDA YOU'RE NEXT
NO YOU GO
I'M STAYING
WHAT? NO!
YES. I'VE KEPT MY PROMISE & LED YOU TO SAFETY
SORRY BUT I NEED TO HELP THE OTHERS
BUT WE CAME HERE TO HELP YOU!
& THAT'S WHY I NEED TO GO BACK! YOU'VE ALWAYS TAUGHT ME TO HELP OTHERS WHEN YOU CAN
& I CAN
ANDROMEDA PLEASE, NO!
I'VE MADE UP MY MIND
BUT I CAN'T LOSE YOU AGAIN!
YOU WONT. TRUST ME. NOW PLEASE GO BACK TO THE SHIP & GET READY FOR US TO LEAVE
YOU'VE TRIED TO KEEP ME SAFE MY ENTIRE LIFE. NOW LET IT BE MY TURN
BUT THERE MUST BE SOMETHING I CAN DO TO HELP
IF YOU REALLY WANT TO HELP TELL ME HOW TO REMOVE THESE?
AL 15

OW! MOM!?
HOLD STILL. YOU'VE HAD WORSE
ONE.. TWO..
THERE YA GO! HMM..INCREDIBLE ACTUALLY QUITE A SIMPLE NEURAL RELAY LINK, LOOK
ER YES AMAZING ...& REALLY GROSS!
NOW SHOW ME HOW TO DO THAT AS I NEED TO DISCONNECT A LOT OF THEM
NOT WHEN THEY'RE ACTIVE YOU CAN'T, IT WOULD BE TOO DANGEROUS
YOU NEED TO BREAK THE SIGNAL FIRST THEN THEY'LL JUST DISCONNECT THEMSELVES EVENTUALLY
THIS THING HAS ONLY A VERY SMALL RANGE
GIVEN THE THICKNESS OF THOSE WALLS THE CORRIDORS SHOULD BE FAR ENOUGH AWAY FROM THE META ROOMS
BUT THE MACHINES WONT LET THEM LEAVE!
SO COME BACK WITH ME
I WILL, BUT FIRST I WANT TO AT LEAST DO WHAT I CAN
OK. IF YOU'RE DETERMINED TO DO THIS
I CAN KEEP THE MACHINES BUSY. I'LL ENTER AN OVERRIDE COMMAND BACK AT THE SHIP
WHEN YOU SEE THE MACHINES ALL LEAVING AT THE SAME TIME TELL YOUR FRIENDS TO START MOVING EVERYONE THROUGH THE EXITS
NOT SURE HOW LONG YOU'LL HAVE
JUST DO WHAT YOU CAN THEN GET OUT OF THERE
I'LL BE WAITING

CASSY COULDN'T LEAVE THOUGH
NOT WITHOUT ONE MORE IDEA
ONE MORE PLAN
ONE MORE OFFER OF HELP
HEY ALIS THROW ME YOUR GOGGLES
A SLIGHTLY CONFUSED ALIS DID SO
THERE
ER THANKS MOM.. ..WHAT HAVE YOU DONE TO THEM?
THEY'VE GOT AN UPGRADE
WHEN YOU ARE IN SIGNAL RANGE THE GOGGLES WILL NOW SHOW YOU WHATEVER THE GUESTS SEE!
COOL!
IT MIGHT BE HELPFUL
OK GOING
CANAPÉ BRING HER BACK SAFE

WHAT TOOK YOU? I WAS GETTING WORRIED
IS ALIS OK?
DID YOU GIVE HER YOUR GUN?
SHE'LL BE JOINING US LATER
NO POINT I DRAINED IT WHEN I CHARGED THAT DROID
JETTISON
WASTE
AWW YOU GAVE UP YOUR GUN FOR CANAPE!
YOU'RE NOT AS TOUGH AS YOU MAKE OUT!
SHUT UP WE HAVE WORK TO DO
YES CASSIOPEIA OF COURSE CASSIOPEIA
OK OK YOU CAN CALL ME CASSY
NOW STAND STILL I NEED TO CAPTURE YOUR IMAGE
OK, NOW TO ADD SOME CODING
RIGHT WE ARE GOING FISHING!

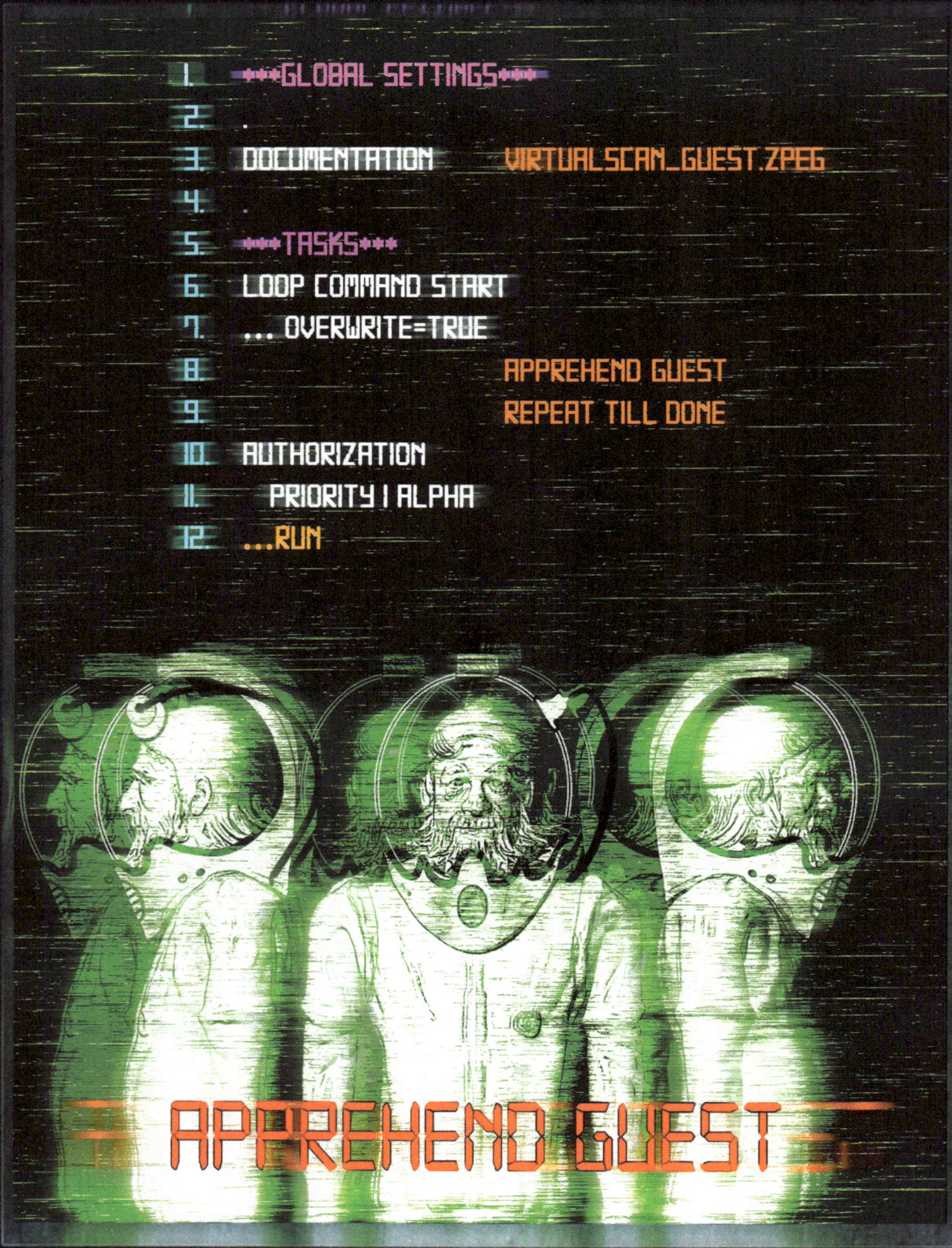
1. ***GLOBAL SETTINGS***
2. .
3. DOCUMENTATION VIRTUALSCAN_GUEST.ZPEG
4. .
5. ***TASKS***
6. LOOP COMMAND START
7. ... OVERWRITE=TRUE
8. APPREHEND GUEST
9. REPEAT TILL DONE
10. AUTHORIZATION
11. PRIORITY I ALPHA
12. ...RUN
APPREHEND GUEST

ALIS AND HER METAL COMPANION QUICKLY MADE THEIR WAY BACK THROUGH THE WILD JUNGLE FIGURING THAT IF THE INSECTS HAD ANY SENSE AT ALL THEY WOULDN'T ATTACK AGAIN WITH CANAPÉ AROUND! AND INDEED THEY DIDN'T
BACK THROUGH THE META MOUNTAINS ROOM WHERE THE SAME COUPLE WERE STILL TRYING TO SCALE THE MOUNTAIN THAT WASN'T REALLY THERE PLUS A CHANCE TO TEST THE GOGGLES
VERY SOON THEY WERE AT THE PLACE WHERE THE DISCONNECTED HAD LEFT HER EARLIER
THE RAFT WAS MOORED UP BUT THERE WAS NO ONE TO BE SEEN
I'M BACK! ALIS SHOUTED
YOU'RE HERE SOMEWHERE! I KNOW YOU ARE!
I'VE KEPT MY PROMISE AND I LED THE OTHERS TO SAFETY
THE RAINS HAVE STARTED! AND WE HAVE A PLAN
I'LL KEEP SHOUTING UNTIL YOU COME OUT!
IT'S A GREAT PLAN!

THE CREW OF THE RAFT STEPPED OUT OF THE SHADOWS
SADNESS AND LOST HOPE ETCHED ON THEIR FACES

MANY PLANS HAVE COME AND FAILED BEFORE
YOU SHOULDN'T HAVE COME BACK
IT'S NOT SAFE TO BE HERE

I CAME BACK BECAUSE IT'S NOT SAFE TO BE HERE
AND I KNOW WE CAN BEAT THIS!

NOT THAT THEY HAD THE CHOICE BUT THEY DID LISTEN TO ALI5' PLAN
SHE SPOKE WITH SUCH DETERMINATION THAT THEY STARTED TO BELIEVE
IT ACTUALLY COULD HAPPEN

A QUIET HOPE WAS BEGINNING TO BE DARED FOR ONCE MORE

AS ALI5 SPOKE QUIET HOPE TURNED INTO CURIOSITY
IF THEY COULD SAVE JUST A FEW LIVES
IT WOULD BE WORTH THE FAITH
THEY WERE ABOUT TO PLACE IN HER

SOON A STRATEGY WAS BEING FORMULATED

THEY AGREED TO GATHER THE DISCONNECTED

SOME WOULD GO INTO THE META ROOMS AND LOOK FOR A WAY
TO INFLUENCE THE GUESTS TO BE CLOSE TO THE EXITS
WHETHER THAT WAS BY KNOCKING OVER TABLES,
SPILLING DRINKS, PLACING OBSTACLES IN THE WAY TO GUIDE THEM,
ANYTHING THAT MIGHT WORK

SOME WOULD BE AT THE EXITS TO PHYSICALLY MOVE THE GUESTS THROUGH
IF AND ONLY WHEN IT WAS SAFE TO DO SO

THE REST WERE TO STATION THEMSELVES IN THE CORRIDORS
TO RECEIVE ANYONE WHO POSSIBLY CAME THROUGH
AND HELP THEM THROUGH THE CONFUSING TRANSITION
THEY WOULD BE BOUND TO EXPERIENCE

AND ALI5? ALI5 WOULD DO WHATEVER SHE COULD

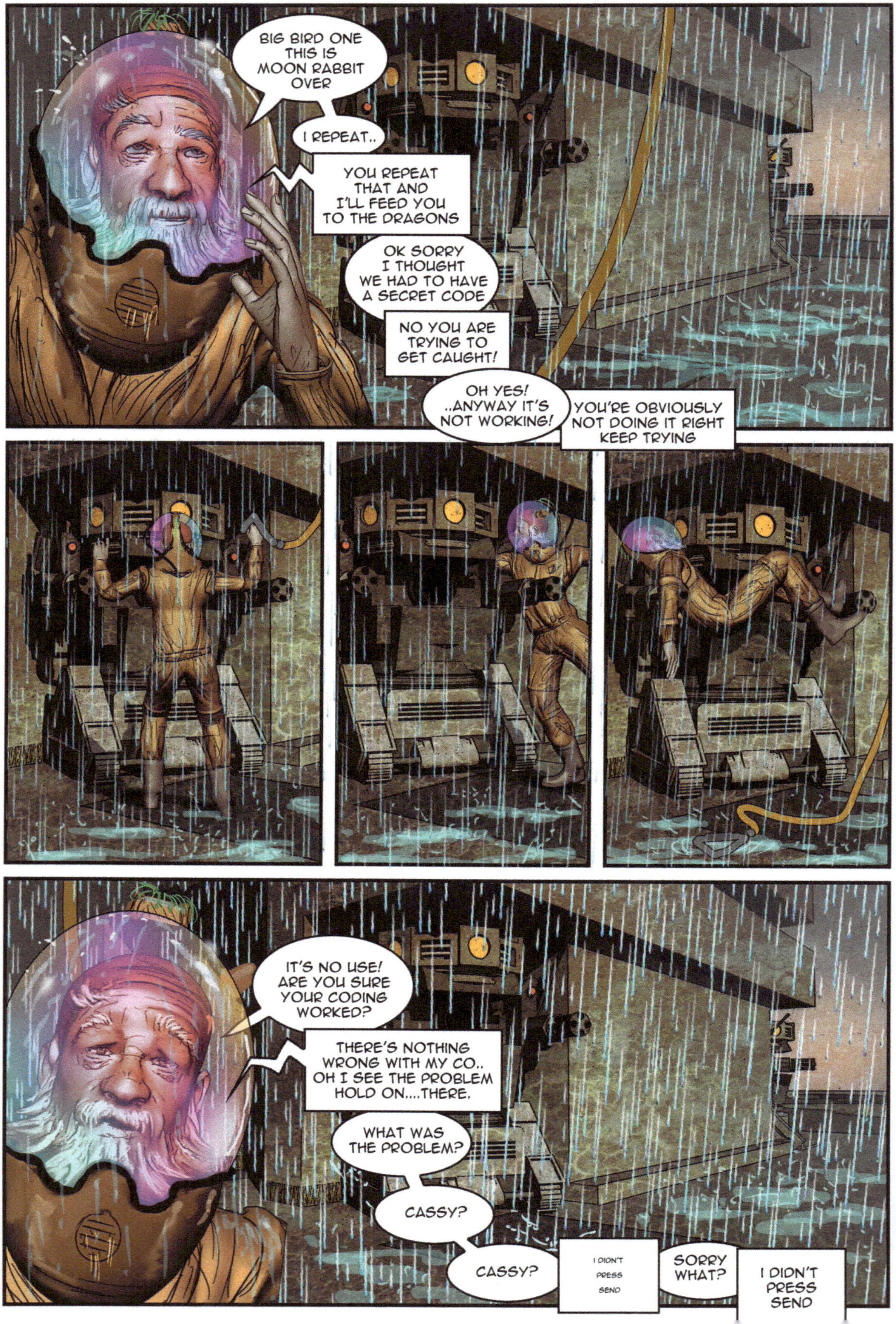

BIG BIRD ONE THIS IS MOON RABBIT OVER
I REPEAT..
YOU REPEAT THAT AND I'LL FEED YOU TO THE DRAGONS
OK SORRY I THOUGHT WE HAD TO HAVE A SECRET CODE
NO YOU ARE TRYING TO GET CAUGHT!
OH YES! ..ANYWAY IT'S NOT WORKING!
YOU'RE OBVIOUSLY NOT DOING IT RIGHT KEEP TRYING
IT'S NO USE! ARE YOU SURE YOUR CODING WORKED?
THERE'S NOTHING WRONG WITH MY CO.. OH I SEE THE PROBLEM HOLD ON....THERE.
WHAT WAS THE PROBLEM?
CASSY?
CASSY?
I DIDN'T PRESS SEND
SORRY WHAT?
I DIDN'T PRESS SEND

ARE YOU SURE THIS IS THE ROOM I WAS KEPT IN? IT'S NOT VERY FAMILIAR
COOEE AL15!
AH OK YES IT IS
HI..OH WOW NOT WHAT I EXPECTED
AL 15
WHAT? MY LITTLE OUTFIT? YES I KNOW STUNNING ISN'T IT?
ER, YES IT'S VERY SHINY
THANK YOU SO SWEET
BETWEEN YOU AND ME THOUGH IT'S A NIGHTMARE TO WALK IN! LIKE WADING THROUGH WATER
STILL ONE HAS TO SUFFER FOR HIGH COUTURE
AND YOU LOOK ... ACCEPTABLE

DEFINITELY GETTING THEIR ATTENTION NOW!
FANTASTIC!
YOU'D BEST PULL ME UP A BIT

WHEN I'VE ATTACHED THE ROPE!!!
ZUGZWANG MEGALOPOLIS

WHAT? OH NO I'D FORGOTTEN ABOUT THIS THING!
HEY WAIT! I HAVEN'T TAKEN MY DRINK YET!
THAT'S THE THIRD BOT TO IGNORE ME IN THE PAST MINUTE!
IT HAS STARTED!
I NEED TO TELL YOU SOMETHING REALLY IMPORTANT
YOU KNOW ME ALIS ALWAYS LISTENING
YOU'RE TRAPPED AND IN GREAT DANGER!
CALL THEMSELVES DRINKS BOTS!
EVERYTHING IS NOT WHAT YOU THINK IT IS
THEY'RE JUST ONE STEP AWAY FROM A TOASTER
YOU NEED TO COME WITH ME THROUGH THE MAZE NOW!
AT LEAST 'THEY' GIVE YOU TOAST WHEN YOU WANT IT
I CAN SAVE YOU!
RIGHT I MUST FIND THAT DRINK
ARE YOU EVEN LISTENING TO ME?
OF COURSE DEAR 'PLAY IN THE MAZE WITH ME YAK A DEE YA'
AL 15
NOW WE DON'T WANT TO MISS GEROME'S VIRTUAL MESSAGE COME ON!
OH CANAPÉ WHAT DO I DO? SHE'LL NEVER HEAR THE TRUTH NOT IN TIME
AHH.. IF THEY WONT LISTEN TO TRUTHS.. I'LL HAVE TO PLAY THEIR GAME! THANKS CANAPÉ
I'VE BEEN ASKED TO GET YOU FOR A SURPRISE PARTY IN YOUR HONOR ..BY GEROME THE ACTUAL GEROME AND IT'S THROUGH THE MAZE
OH HOW EXCITING THIS IS MY LUCKY DAY!
I'LL GO AND GET EVERYONE ELSE TO HELP ME CELEBRATE BESIDES THEY'LL BE GREEN WITH ENVY!
OH AND DON'T YOU WORRY I'LL BE SURE TO BE 'TOTALLY SURPRISED'!
I'M SURE YOU WILL BE
WELL THAT WORKED BETTER THAN I HOPED! SHE'LL NOT BE LEAVING ANYBODY BEHIND!
I KNOW IT'S NOT REAL BUT THIS DRESS STILL REALLY ANNOYS ME!

NOW I KNOW WHAT THE FISH HEAD FELT LIKE!
WE'LL GET THEM FAR ENOUGH AWAY TO GIVE ALIS SUFFICIENT TIME THEN I'LL DELETE THE CODE
OK DELETE THE CODE?
A BIT FURTHER

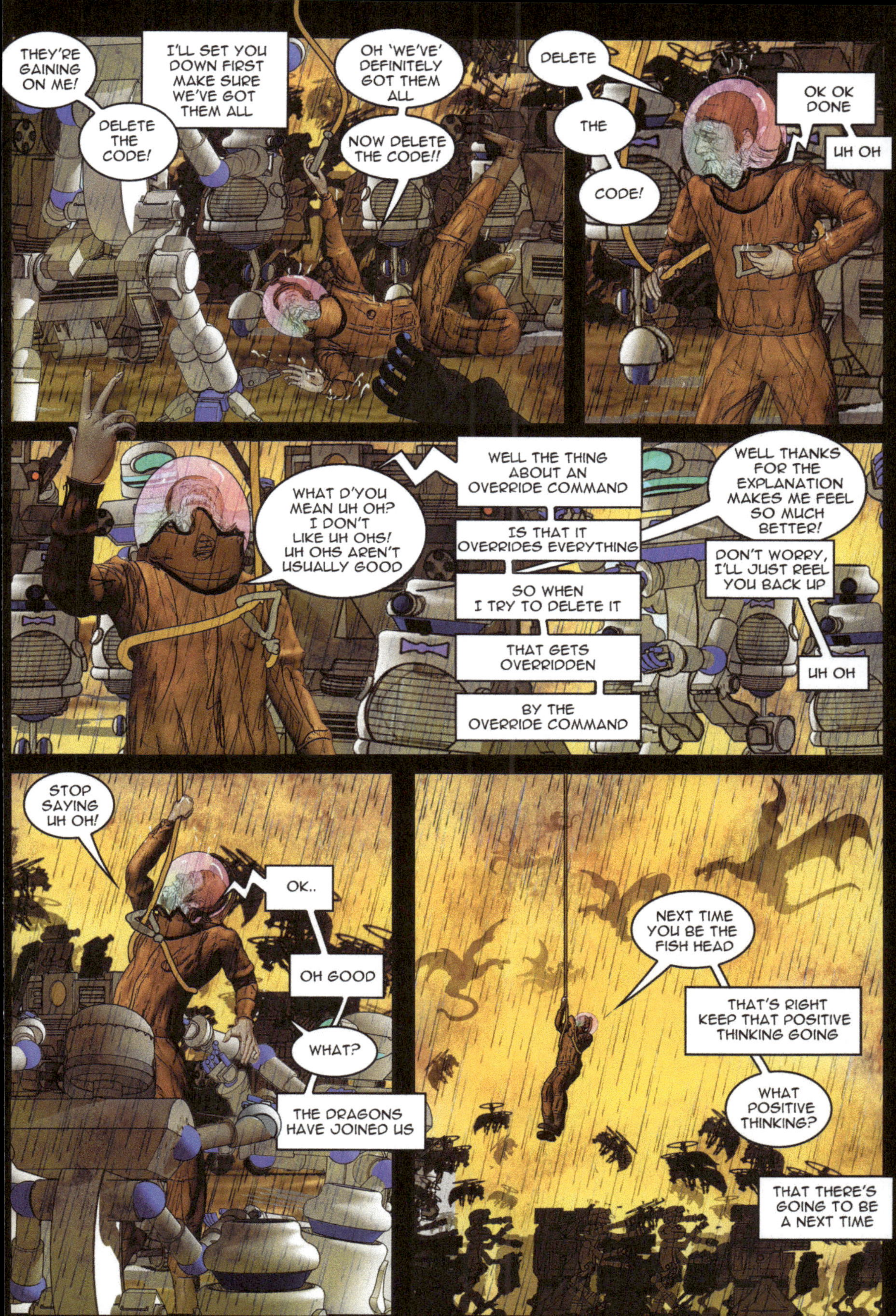

THEY'RE GAINING ON ME!
I'LL SET YOU DOWN FIRST MAKE SURE WE'VE GOT THEM ALL
DELETE THE CODE!
OH 'WE'VE' DEFINITELY GOT THEM ALL
NOW DELETE THE CODE!!
DELETE
THE
CODE!
OK OK DONE
UH OH
WHAT D'YOU MEAN UH OH? I DON'T LIKE UH OHS! UH OHS AREN'T USUALLY GOOD
WELL THE THING ABOUT AN OVERRIDE COMMAND
IS THAT IT OVERRIDES EVERYTHING
SO WHEN I TRY TO DELETE IT
THAT GETS OVERRIDDEN
BY THE OVERRIDE COMMAND
WELL THANKS FOR THE EXPLANATION MAKES ME FEEL SO MUCH BETTER!
DON'T WORRY, I'LL JUST REEL YOU BACK UP
UH OH
STOP SAYING UH OH!
OK..
OH GOOD
WHAT?
THE DRAGONS HAVE JOINED US
NEXT TIME YOU BE THE FISH HEAD
THAT'S RIGHT KEEP THAT POSITIVE THINKING GOING
WHAT POSITIVE THINKING?
THAT THERE'S GOING TO BE A NEXT TIME

ONCE MORE SHALL I BECOME VICTORIOUS
& CLAIM MY RIGHTFUL PLACE AMONGST THE CHAMPIONS OF ATLANTIS
HA!
YOUR CHALLENGE IS ACCEPTED
MAY HAKATAR SMITE YOUR JOURNEY
NO
I HAVE THE STAFF OF VALOR TO CLEAR MY WAY
WAIT!! THAT ONE HAS NO STEED!
ATLANTIAN WHERE IS YOUR STEED?
HOW MAY YOU EVEN HOPE TO COMPETE?

I AM THE EMISSARY TO THE GATE-KEEPER ..PERSON
I HAVE JOURNEYED FAR TO BRING YOU A DECLARATION OF HIGH IMPORTANCE
THIS RACE MUST HEREBY DISCONTINUE & CEASE
NEEDS MUST YOU FOLLOW ME TO THE.. SHRINE ..OF PLENTY
..YOU WILL BE REWARDED WITH GRATITUDE & GIFTS?
I DONT THINK THEY'RE BUYING IT!
TELL US EMISSARY, WHAT WONDEROUS GIFTS AWAIT US?
OH LOTS OF WONDEROUS.. THINGS & CAKE COME, I WILL GUIDE YOU ALL ..FORTHWITH

THEY ARE FOLLOWING
FANTASTIC! NOW HEAD FOR THE EXIT CANAPÉ
& LET'S HOPE THE NEXT ROOM IS EASIER!
INDEED
FORWARD ATLANTIANS THE STAFF OF VALOR WILL KEEP US SAFE!

OPERATION ALIS, AS IT WOULD LATER COME TO BE KNOWN, WAS WORKING. CONFUSED GUESTS WERE STARTING TO EMERGE FROM THEIR META CELLS GREETED BY FAMILIAR, IF SLIGHTLY BLURRED, FACES
THE DISCONNECTED HAD ORGANIZED THEMSELVES FORMING LINES TO SAFETY EACH REASSURINGLY DEBRIEFING THE GUESTS AS THEY PASSED

MEANWHILE
MARCUS HAD MANAGED TO SAFELY BOARD THE SHIP WITHOUT GETTING EATEN THIS WAS PROBABLY DUE TO HIS SUIT NOT GIVING OFF ANY EDIBLE ODORS ALTHOUGH MARCUS WAS CONVINCED IT WAS BECAUSE HE KEPT HIS LIGHTS OFF AND THEY JUST COULDN'T SEE HIM
LOOK! A WORMHOLE IS STARTING TO OPEN!
WE NEED TO GET BACK TO THE CITY & PICK UP ALIS! WE'RE ON OUR WAY HOME!
I'LL SIGNAL CANAPÉ NOW
OH I'M SURE I CAN SHAKE OFF THE DRAGONS
WHAT ABOUT THE DRAGONS? & THOSE MACHINES?
AND THE MACHINES WONT BE A PROBLEM. WE'LL BE LONG GONE BEFORE THEY MANAGE TO WALK BACK

SAVINGS BANK
YOU HEARDS WHAT THE LIL LADY SAID NTO THE VAULT YOUS GUYS
TEXAS-1933 587 956
INCOMING MESSAGE
ALIS TIME IS UP RETURN TO THE SHIP NOW
OK ALMOST THERE. JUST ONE MORE ROOM LEFT
THAT'S REMARKABLE! DID NOT KNOW L THE MACHINES OULD BE ABLE TO FLY
I THOUGHT YOU KNEW THOSE KIND OF THINGS?
SORRY BUT I DIDN'T SPECIALIZE IN MANIACAL ROBOTS. NOT MUCH CALL FOR IT ON VIRIDI
TELL ME THEY CAN'T GET IN?
THEY CAN'T GET IN
NOT FOR A WHILE AT LEAST
INSIDE, ALIS HAD BECOME A DREAMWALKER, ADOPTING THE AVATAR OF WHATEVER CHARACTER WOULD HELP MOVE THOSE GUESTS TOWARDS THE EXIT. OUTSIDE, THE FORCE OF THE ELECTRIC STORM HAD DRIED UP THE RAINS AS BEASTS AND MACHINES ALIKE ATACKED THE INTREPID DECOYS

SWEETHEART WE HAVE MADE IT!
IT LOOKS DESERTED
THERE'S GOT TO BE SOMEONE HERE!
DO WE JUST KNOCK?
NO NEED THE DOOR'S OPENING!
THERE YOU ARE! TOOK YOU LONG ENOUGH
PLEASE WE NEED SHEL...
YES YES COME IN QUICKLY
FOLLOW ME

THANK YOU SHOULD WE TAKE OFF OUR BOOTS? OR LIGHT A CANDLE OR SOMETHING?
I DON'T CARE
OK.. SO WE GOT CAUGHT IN THIS AVALANCHE..
AH BUT DID YOU?
WHAT IS THIS PLACE? THERE'S NOTHING IN HERE
THIS INSIDE HAS NO STORY
YOU WERE NOT MEANT TO GET THIS FAR
THAT'S SO DEEP! WE ARE VERY GRATEFUL! YOU ARE A LIFE SAVER!
I NEEDED TO SAVE YOU BEFORE I COULD SAVE MYSELF
NOW GO THROUGH THAT DOORWAY AND MY TIME HERE IS DONE
THANK Y..OH HE'S GONE
WHAT A WISE & SPIRITUAL OLD MAN!
BEN?
HUNNY LOOK!!!
IT'S BEN!
HELLO DAD, MOM

AT LEAST I CAN SEE THE DRAGONS ARE GOING!
GOOD EVENING INSERT SIR I HAVE COME TO GIVE YOU A HELPING HAND
GOING WHERE?
OH NO IT'S ALIS SHE'S COMING OUT & THEY'RE HEADING STRAIGHT FOR HER!
WE'RE GOING IN TO GET HER
BUT THEY'VE ALMOST BROKEN IN!
YOU'RE RIGHT, I NEED TO SHAKE THE MACHINES OFF FIRST
DID YOU HAVE ANY LUNCH?
NO?
GOOD BECAUSE THAT REALLY WOULDN'T BE NICE TO SEE. HOLD ON!
WOOOAAHHH

WHAT? NO I'M TOO LATE!
AT LEAST EVERYONE'S SAFE NOW
NO CANAPÉ MOVE OUT OF HARM'S WAY
YOU CAN'T HELP THIS TIME BUDDY
& NO PEACE OFFERINGS THIS TIME EITHER!

AS ALIS FACED THE DRAGONS A TERRIFYING SCREECH FROM ABOVE STOPPED THEM IN THEIR TRACKS!
BY THE SHADOW HOVERING OVER THEM WHATEVER THEY WERE FEARFUL OF WAS ABOUT TO LAND. THE DRAGONS TOOK SEVERAL STEPS BACKWARDS AS THOUGH TO OBSERVE THE RESPECTFUL DISTANCE THEY HAD SHOWN TO THE ALPHA EARLIER ON. BUT THIS WAS DIFFERENT. THIS CLEARLY AGITATED THEM.

WITH FEROCIOUS SPEED, A CRIMSON DRAGON SEEMINGLY SUPERCHARGED BY THE STORM RELEASED ITS FULL FURY.. ON THE ATTACKERS
THE DRAGONS BELOW SCATTERED AS FLAMES FORCED THEM BACK ALIS FIGURED IT WAS DEMANDING THE FIRST BITE AND THAT SHE WOULD BE NEXT ALTHOUGH, SHE THOUGHT, ONE ADVERSARY IS FAR FAIRER THAN MANY
COME ON THEN! LET'S GET THIS OVER WITH!
CLENCHING THE ONLY ROCK SHE COULD FIND
BUT AS THE DRAGON TURNED TO HER IT JUST STARED AND LET OUT A FAMILIAR WHIMPER SOUND
WHAT? NO ?!
...LITTLE RED?
LITTLE RED? IS THAT YOU???

IT TASTES BETTER THAN IT LOOKS, HONEST
THERE LITTLE RED.. YOU'RE NOT SO TOUGH
IT IS YOU! HOW DID YOU GET HERE YOU POOR THING ?
AWW THANK LITTLE RE APPRECIATED
FRESH
LITTLE RED!! THANK YOU!
HOW HAVE YOU GROWN SO MUCH?
GUESS YOU MUST HAVE ESCAPED THROUGH A WORMHOLE TOO HUH?
I'M SO GLAD YOU'RE SAFE
AND KINDA IN CHARGE HUH?
AL 15

IF EVER IT WERE POSSIBLE FOR MACHINES TO BECOME RILED FOR NOT BEING ABLE TO COMPLETE THEIR TASK, THIS WAS IT
THEY SURE DON'T GIVE UP EASY!
WELL NEITHER DO I!
MARCUS PLAN B
I'M NOT EVEN GOING TO ASK
INCOMING MESSAGE
ALIS MAKE FOR THE CLEARING, WE'RE COMING IN FAST
OH WOW THEY DIDN'T LEAVE US BEHIND!
LITTLE RED KEEP YOUR FRIENDS AWAY FOR A LITTLE WHILE LONGER?

C'MON CANAPÉ THIS WAY!
ALIS LOOK BEHIND YOU

GOT THEM!
GO GO GO
HEY
MARCUS
SO GOOD TO
SEE YOU!

THE
WORMHOLE'S
CLOSING!
WE CAN
MAKE IT!
PROBABLY

..SIX..
..SEVEN..
..EIGHT..

THE END
& DON'T THINK I'VE FORGOTTEN ABOUT YOUR DAD'S BOOTS
IT'S OK I'VE GOT THEM SAFE
..WHAT HAPPENED TO YOUR DAD?
... LONG STORY

ALIS 2

NEW YEARS
Design
Entrance
service lift
3'6" long
5' 2"
(1.57m)
3' 9" resting
4'6" active
can extend to 6'6"
6' stance
extends to 7'6"
7' tall
6' max wide
Scale
Machines
Chess Inspired
Pawn
service droids

Rook
SECURITY
Bishop
Knight

Makeshift Raft design
lashed together piping
over joists base
canopy
storage
storage
rudder
pedal-power
paddles
floor made of door,
panels & planks
light
for hanging
fishing net
canopy
pipe & rope rails
storage
storage
pedal-power
paddles
barrels 4 x 3
rudder

Research
Bonnie & Clyde Scene

Continuity

Ageing Little Red

from Youth to young Adult

dominant but still friendly?

extend snout, nostrils & horns add lips

keep
cheeks
smile
colors (obvs)

larger eyes than others

Original

horns & teeth friendlier than others

For Barbara

For......................

I hope you've enjoyed the book. It was a huge amount of fun to create.

I decided early on that this volume has to be dedicated to our mothers: yours (if you've been lucky enough to know them) and mine. After all, if you went missing in a far off land who might be the one person who wouldn't stop looking for you? (then comment on your clothes when they found you). Among too many other things to mention here, my mum Barbara taught me the joy of painting and how to not give up on my dreams.

You wanted more. After the amazing reviews of the first volume, and fully aware of the potential also-ran syndrome of a sequel, I set out to give you more: more in-depth story, action, twists, characters, environments and social commentary, whilst trying to stay true to the first book and moving it forwards. In an effort to keep these pages fresh I've also added more art styles into the mix, letting the pictures tell more of the story than before.

The chief villain in this volume isn't someone you can point a finger at and boo. It is, as it turns out, an algorithm. With the double meaning of 'you deserve it' this dystopian world exists directly as a result of technology deciding what we see, do and buy for the sake of someone else's profit. Whilst travelling through a gravitational wormhole isn't a reality yet - entering a metaverse, using your own personalised avatar and buying digital assets based on your own freely given data has already started.
A cautionary tale of 'accept all cookies'?

Easter egg. Did you notice the weird name on the entrance to the city?
Zugswang is actually a real word. It's a situation taken from chess where every move you do is going to make things worse.. I.e. 'it's a trap and there's nothing you can do about it!'

So, you've seen Green Land (Viridi Terram), Wonder Land (Miror Terram) & now Dream Land (Somnium Terram) Where next? Or possibly when next?

BTW I found it comforting to think that 250 plus years in the future we may still be forgetting to press send!

& a special thanks to Kamila
for the Polish translations Dziękuję

SDeLaMare

Steve De La Mare is a freelance artist, sculptor & visualizer working in the theme park industry with work reaching as far afield as Malaysia, Japan, China, USA, UAE, Germany, Italy, Turkey, Belgium and the UK.

His art can be seen at stevedelamare.artstation.com

LET'S LEARN ABOUT
WORMHOLES
NEW FOR SUMMER 2032
WORLD'S FIRST ENGINEERED WORMHOLE!
NEGATIVE MATTER
Augmented Reality Trips
See for yourself why travelling instantaneously to a point through Exotic Matter that would normally take light years means that you would actually be travelling Backwards in Time!
AUGMENTED LEARNING
SPONSORED BY
PATRIAM CORPORATION
BUILDING FOR YOUR FUTURE
TEMPLE VISION IMPLANTS REQUIRED

CPSIA information can be obtained
at www.ICGtesting.com
Printed in the USA
LVHW071834171022
730902LV00009B/278

9 781915 387707